The band began to play a haunting tune. "Joanna," his voice was muffled against her ear. She looked at him and saw his longing. "Let's get out of here."

She nodded wordlessly. Yesterday was gone and who could know what tomorrow would hold? But she had tonight. She was here with Pete again and there was magic between them as there had always been. She wouldn't think about consequences now. Just for tonight, she would listen to her heart instead of her head.

"Come on." Still holding her hand, he led her across the crowded floor and out to the dark lot where his car was parked.

In the shadows of the gnarled pear tree, he gathered her into his arms and kissed her without restraint.

It was graduation night all over again. Blooms of silver-white formed a scented canopy that enclosed their moonlit world. Tomorrow Pete would be gone; there was only tonight. How could she tell him how much she loved him when words were not enough? Of its own volition her body found a way.

The long kiss ended. In the awed silence that followed, they held each other once again, the long undreamed of separation over.

Praise for Linda Swift's first novel, THAT SPECIAL SUMMER:

"The author motivates thoughts on the delicate balance of life and death, of loss and healing love. In this novel, as in the heroine's life, every moment counts."

~Gail Benninger, Romantic Times

"Linda's mature characters are a joy to read; they are well-rounded and most importantly, they are credible."

~Mary D. Pinto, Affaire de Coeur

Circle of Love

by

Linda Swift

This is a work of fiction. Names, characters, places, and incidents either are the product of the author's imagination or are used fictitiously, and any resemblance to actual persons living or dead, business establishments, events, or locales, is entirely coincidental.

Circle Of Love

Contact Information: info@thewildrosepress.com

Cover Art by *Nicola Martinez*

The Wild Rose Press
PO Box 708
Adams Basin, NY 14410-0706
Visit us at www.thewildrosepress.com

Publishing History
First Last Rose Of Summer Edition, 2008
Print ISBN 1-60154-539-8

Published in the United States of America

Dedication

For Bob, Alan, Kaye, and Wesley,
with special thanks to
Eleanore and Kathi Cramer,
who gave us Circles of Love.

CHAPTER ONE

"Joanna, is it really you?"

"Vada Kirkland. How nice to see you." They embraced warmly.

"I'm Vada Mittendorf now."

Joanna smiled. "As in Mrs. Al Mittendorf?"

"The very same. And you?"

"Still Flemming."

"Oh, I do so want to talk with you and catch up on all the years but I'm in charge here for now." She motioned toward the registration table where several students were checking lists and giving out tickets.

"We're all so glad you could make the reunion this year, Joanna. Just register and get your ticket, then go on in and find a table. Thel and Bets are in there someplace and they're dying to see you. I'll catch up with you later."

Joanna took her ticket from a polite student and turned again toward Vada who was busy greeting others as the crowd pressed forward. She looked the same as she always did except her hair was lighter blond now. Vada, Bets, and Thel. What close friends they had been, moving en masse through their high school years. What one wore, all wore. What one did, all did.

They'd made the pep squad together, then paired off with the A-team basketball players to the envy of every other girl in school. They'd called themselves the Fabulous Four and some of their escapades lived up to their name. Like soaping the windows of the principal's house on Halloween. And hanging toilet paper from the trees in the gym teacher's yard.

It was all harmless fun but Pete had frowned disapproval when they'd confessed their guilt to the boys and collapsed in fits of giggles. "What if your dad found out?" he had whispered sternly. "He might stop you from going out with me."

A large banner proclaiming "WELCOME, GREENVILLE GRADUATES" hung above the gym entrance. Joanna looked around the crowded room. Blue and white balloons floated above the festive tables. And there was even a wishing well. Memories washed over her like a flooding river, taking her breath away. Who would have thought the reunion decorations would be a replica of that prom night so long ago when she and Pete had tossed pennies into the water and sealed their wishes with a furtive kiss. How smitten she had been with the lanky blue-eyed boy who had braved constant disapproval to date the minister's daughter. Most of their time together, except for school events, had been spent sitting in the wicker swing on the front porch of the parsonage under the watchful eye of her strict father. But Pete hadn't seemed to mind as long as they were together.

Her eyes and heart stopped at the head table where Peter Damron and Betsy Hurst stood talking. Feeling weak, she sat down in the nearest chair. Pete's hair had a hint of silver now, but how handsome and distinguished he was. Tears stung her eyes and she blinked and swallowed, then forced herself to look away. She clasped her hands tightly to still their trembling and tried to focus her attention on the floating balloons, but their constant motion made her feel dizzy.

The room was rapidly filling. Then Pete tapped the microphone and greeted the crowd. Joanna closed her eyes and savored the sound of his voice.

"Good evening, graduates, and welcome to this final reunion in honor of the old Greenville High School. Tonight is the result of weeks of planning and work by an excellent committee who graduated in my class, and I've promised not to say how many years ago that was."

When the laughter subsided, he motioned for the three women to stand. "Please give a big round of applause for Betsy Debolt, Vada Mittendorf, and Thelma Bernard."

How like Pete to give most of the credit to someone else. He had always shared equal glory with his teammates for winning the State Basketball Tournament but it had been his unbeatable skill that had sealed the victory for Greenville.

After the room grew quiet, Pete thanked the Home Ec. Class and other students who had helped. He introduced the Board members and mentioned the building of the new school. And finally he called on the town's current Protestant minister to bless the food and sat down.

Joanna was aware of Pete as if he were seated beside her. She went through the motions of eating while her mind absorbed the information she had just learned. Betsy had married Walt DeBolt, forsaking her dreams of moving to a big city. While she, who dreamed of always living in Greenville with Pete, had left and never returned until now. She formed and discarded a hundred ways to say hello to him. Finally as the meal ended, she simply stood and walked toward the front.

Pete was shaking hands with the minister and thanking him for coming when Joanna approached. Leaving his sentence unfinished, he came to meet her.

"Hello, Joanna." He reached to take her hand, paused, then bent to brush her cheek.

Warmth traveled with the speed of light from hand to cheek as flesh touched flesh for one brief moment and left a star-struck girl longing for more.

Standing close enough to feel his breath on her forehead, Joanna answered softly, "Hello, Pete."

"You're as pretty as you ever were."

"Thank you, Pete." His eyes were the same steel blue and she thought he had never looked more handsome. But she didn't know how to say that without sounding intimate.

"Joanna!" Betsy rushed through the crowd and enveloped her in a strong bear hug. "Oh, God, how great to see you after all these years. You haven't changed a bit. Doesn't she look good, Pete?"

Pete grinned at her with frank admiration and said is a low voice, "Damned good."

Thelma and Boyd Bernard stopped to greet them. Then Pete turned to talk with another group of people and Joanna allowed herself to be swept along for one last tour of the old school.

The hallway was dimly lit but Joanna saw the familiar metal lockers lining its walls and caught a ghostly image of the boy and girl who had lingered beside them, reluctant to separate until the next class ended.

Every look that passed between them had been filled with promise. They had known without words that they were meant to be together for always. So how could they have—

"Say, Joanna, remember how you and Pete used to hang around your locker until the last bell rang and—" Boyd's words were interrupted by his wife's quick intervention.

"Honey, why don't you go on ahead and turn on lights in the classrooms? I would have thought they'd have the place all lit up for us."

As soon as her husband was out of ear shot, Thelma turned to Joanna. "I'm sorry about that, Jo. Boyd says things before he thinks sometimes."

"No problem, Thel," she answered with a forced smile, pushing her earlier thoughts to the past where they belonged. "That was then, this is now."

The others had stopped before a trophy case that stood outside the principal's office. Behind its gleaming glass doors were the tangible reminders of the school's athletic teams through the years. And towering above all the rest was the State Championship Trophy won the year Pete was the senior star basketball player.

Betsy struck a pose. "Give me a G, give me an R."

Thelma joined in. "Give me an E,E, N."

Vada rushed up and grabbed Joanna's arm, pulling her to the front. Laughing, she finished the cheer with them. "Give me a V. Give me an I, give me an L, L, E. Greenville. Greenville. Greenville."

They clapped and whistled and cheered, clearly caught up in the nostalgic moment in time.

"Oh, lord, I think I've strained something," Thelma groaned, clutching her back. "I probably won't be able to walk tomorrow."

"We're not as young as we once were, Thel," Vada giggled. "High jinks may have to be omitted from our routine."

"I hadn't planned on repeating this act any time soon," Betsy added emphatically.

"Well, why not?" Joanna asked. "I think we're as good as ever."

"Are you insinuating we were *never* any good?" Betsy asked in an injured tone and the four women locked arms and dissolved in laughter.

Just like old times. Joanna's heart swelled with happy memories. The Fabulous Four together as always.

"Ah, those were the days." Vada sighed. "Pete Damron was the greatest forward the school ever had."

"And with the rest of our guys, the team was unbeatable," Betsy added with a smile toward Al and Boyd.

"Remember those long rides home in the dark bus?" Thelma asked.

"And how." Boyd leered at his wife with a playful expression and hugged her close.

Joanna closed her eyes, remembering the feel of Pete's arm around her, the rough texture of the letter on his school jacket as she laid her cheek against his chest. Feeling the steady rhythm of his heartbeat. And the way he nudged her chin up until their lips met in a slow kiss that tasted of salt from their combined dried perspiration. His free hand touching her throat, moving lower but stopping short of touching her breast.

The group continued their tour, reminiscing at every stop in turn. When they came to the English classroom, Joanna lingered after the others moved on. Her old desk was near the back and Pete sat behind her. She easily identified it by their initials which he had carved into its worn wooden top. She stood, unconsciously tracing the letters as she remembered how she had gazed at the pear tree outside the window and dreamed a future life with Pete. Her eyes brimmed with unshed tears and she sighed with resignation. Some things were never meant to be.

"How have you been, Joanna?"

Startled out of her reverie, she answered with a quick intake of breath. "All right. And you, Pete?"

"It's been a good life," he said, "but I've often wondered what could have been."

"Don't," she said softly.

"Joanna, Pete," someone called from the doorway, "we're going on to the gym now. We'll save you a place."

Joanna turned back to Pete. "Betsy says your daughter teaches the Home Ec. classes now."

He nodded, smiling proudly.

"That's nice. I'd like to meet her."

"I have four kids here tonight. I'd like you to meet all of them. There's one more but Michael's in seminary."

Pete, a father. To five children. Someone else had mentioned earlier that his wife had died. She tried to speak but no sound came out. Finally, she managed to stammer something appropriate just as another of their classmates joined them.

"Hey, Pete. There you are. We need to talk about taking pictures of the old school for the archives." Pete became engulfed in discussion about a photo shoot before the building was torn down. Joanna went back to the gym alone.

Walking between the buildings, she thought again of Pete as he was now. Father of grownup children. School Board Chairman. Prosperous farmer. He had made a successful life in Greenville. A good life, by his own admission. Just as she had succeeded in her own sphere of existence. She had earned a place of respect among her peers in education. And although not with the same camaraderie as the Fabulous Four, she had a circle of wonderful friends. It was only the children...she left the thought unfinished as she entered the gym and walked toward the table where her classmates sat.

"Where's Pete?" Betsy asked as she made room for Joanna to sit beside her.

"Talking to someone about photos."

"Do you have any plans for after the banquet?"

Joanna shook her head.

"Come home with me. There's plenty of extra room and we have a lot of years to catch up on. We'll have a slumber party."

Joanna looked at Betsy's expectant face and knew she didn't have the heart to say no. "A slumber party? Like old times when we stayed awake all night eating chocolate and discussing boys and makeup?"

Betsy laughed. "And making out. Though we didn't have a clue what it really meant."

"If you're sure it's no bother, I'd love to stay over. It will be great fun."

"No bother at all. The house gets lonely since Walt died and all the kids are gone."

"I'm sorry I didn't know about his accident until now, Betsy." Joanna squeezed her hand. "I would have come for the service."

"Yeah, well, we didn't know where to locate you. But we finally put our heads together and thought of tracking you down through the college so we could let you know about tonight."

"I should have kept in touch but I...well, I got caught up in getting a degree and beginning a teaching career, and time just slipped away." She felt the need to say something more but what was there she could say to explain all the silent years?

Just then the music began. Betsy and Joanna tried to talk above the noise but finally gave up. When the band began a faster number, Boyd Bernard came back to the table.

"Come on, Bets, dance with me."

"Ah, Boyd, I never could move that fast. Dance with Joanna and save a slow one for me."

"Joanna?"

She got up, smiling. "Sure, I'd love to." The music was throbbing through her veins and she abandoned her usual reticence and gave herself up to the pulsating rhythm.

The song ended and the band segued into a slower beat.

"Will you dance with me, Joanna?" Pete asked, from behind her.

Wordlessly, she turned and accepted his hand. He put his arm around her waist, her arm slid automatically to his broad shoulder and time and place became meaningless.

"I like your dress. Reminds me of what you were wearing the night of our graduation." He smiled at her.

She smiled back. "I'm surprised you remembered. That was a long time ago."

"I've never forgotten...anything about that night."

"Nor I," she told him truthfully.

They danced in silence, each acutely aware of the other in every step they took together, in every place their bodies touched.

"I've missed you, Joanna." Her name was a caress on his tongue.

"Don't," she said, feeling the pleasure-pain in every cell in her body.

"Have you missed me?"

"I've missed you."

"Why didn't you answer my letters?"

She drew a quick breath as she thought of finding Pete's letters in a locked drawer in her father's study after his sudden death. Letters with a familiar looped scrawl that bore foreign stamps, now faded with time. She felt again the sharp pain his words of love and promise had brought. The frustration that caused her to pound her father's immaculate desk in a screaming rage that bruised her doubled fists.

"It doesn't matter now."

"Maybe not." His words sounded unconvinced.

The night, the music, the man who held her

seemed unreal to Joanna but the intense aching inside was very real.

The band began to play a haunting tune. “Joanna.” His voice was muffled against her ear. She looked at him and saw his longing. “Let’s get out of here.”

She nodded wordlessly. Yesterday was gone and who could know what tomorrow would hold? But she had tonight. She was here with Pete again and there was magic between them as there had always been. She wouldn’t think about consequences now. Just for tonight, she would listen to her heart instead of her head.

“Come on.” Still holding her hand, he led her across the crowded floor and out to the dark lot where his car was parked.

In the shadows of the gnarled pear tree, he gathered her into his arms and kissed her without restraint.

It was graduation night all over again. Blooms of silver-white formed a scented canopy that enclosed their moonlit world. Tomorrow Pete would be gone; there was only tonight. How could she tell him how much she loved him when words were not enough? Of its own volition her body found a way.

The long kiss ended. In the awed silence that followed, they held each other once again, the long undreamed of separation over.

CHAPTER TWO

"We need to talk," Pete finally said in a husky voice.

"Shouldn't we have talked before?" Joanna asked wryly as she fitted her head in the familiar hollow between his neck and shoulder.

"Maybe not. First things first." He gently stroked her face. "When I saw you tonight it was like this was where we came in and all the years between us just fell away. Did you feel that, too?"

"Yes," she whispered and tears rolled slowly down her cheeks onto Pete's hand.

He cupped her chin and brushed her lips with his. "Don't cry, Joanna. This is a night to be happy." When she didn't answer, he spoke again. "Let's get in the car and talk. We've got a lot of catching up to do." He opened the door for her, went around to the other side and got behind the wheel. "Betsy said you went to Lambuth. Then what?"

"Then I taught English in high school. A few years ago I went to Peabody and got my doctorate and now I'm teaching at Memphis State." She wiped at her eyes to clear the tears.

"So you're *Doctor* Flemming now? I'm impressed."

"I didn't do this to impress people. It was a matter of better job security and more income."

"And?"

"And there's not much else to tell. I've lived in Tennessee all these years, traveled a little, and looked after my parents until my father died and my mother became so disoriented she had to have constant care."

"Then you've been with them always?"

"Always."

Pete nodded, then said quietly, "I didn't know about your parents. When did this happen?"

"Before I went to Peabody. My father died of a stroke and my mother developed dementia soon after."

"I'm sorry to hear that, Joanna. She was—is a wonderful lady."

"*Was* is right. I feel as if I've lost her, too." Joanna sighed, then changed the subject. "Now what about you?"

"Well, I came back here from the army. You know the rest, marriage, five kids, a farm of my own, serving on the School Board."

"What was it like, Pete? The war, I mean."

He took a deep breath. "That's hard to explain. It was a whole different world, Joanna. I was just a kid who'd won a few ballgames and thought he was a big shot. Then I found myself facing bullets and life wasn't a game anymore. And my girl back home wasn't answering my letters and I couldn't figure out why."

She started to speak but changed her mind.

"It seemed like an eternity until I got leave to come home. And that's when I found out you'd moved to Tennessee. I thought maybe that was why you hadn't written—that you'd never gotten the mail I'd sent."

There was a long pause while he dealt with his painful memories but she remained silent.

"So I went to Jackson and finally found your house." He stopped, clenched his fists. "Your father saw to it I didn't find *you.*"

"I didn't know," she said contritely.

He went on in a monotone. "I came back to Greenville and that was when I first went out with Mary Esther. She was a Junior then, and a cheerleader. After I went back, she wrote to me and by the time I came home to stay I had decided to marry her. I was sick of all the fighting and killing and I wanted a life that meant something. I wanted a wife and kids and a farm of my own." He looked at her with resignation. "You see, I had finally made peace with the fact that I would never have you and that other life we'd dreamed together. Do you understand that?"

"Yes," she answered honestly. "I made a peace of my own in time and tried never to look back, either—until now."

They remained lost in their own thoughts of the past until she broke the silence. "Betsy told me about your wife. I'm sorry."

"Yeah, I don't guess you'd remember Mary Esther. She was only in tenth grade when we graduated."

"I remember her, a petite girl with long black hair. She was very pretty."

"Yeah, she was, before the cancer."

"I'm sorry, Pete," Joanna said again. It was easy to be sympathetic toward Pete's wife—dead. It wouldn't have been easy to see Pete with a living wife. What a chance she'd taken, coming here, not knowing.

Pete cleared his throat. "It was hell watching her fight it so long and lose in the end. She was"—his voice faltered—, "very brave and she wanted to live, for all of us. She was a good wife and mother to our children. We had a good life together, our kids, then the in-laws and our grands. We bought a small farm but added land and built a larger house as time went by. Then our luck ran out."

Joanna put her hand over Pete's. "It must have been very hard for all of you to lose her," she said with sincere sympathy.

"That's over now. And I guess it's time to live again." He reached out to cover her hand with his. "At least, tonight I began to think so for the first time."

"I'm glad," she answered softly.

He raised her hand to his lips, kissed her open palm. After a moment he said, "I never forgot graduation night, making love here in this very place with you. I thought a lot about it while I was away and since. And I've wondered if you remembered, too."

"Every day."

"I don't know whether to be happy or sad to hear you say that." He pulled her into his arms, kissed her deeply. "There's so much we have to talk about and not time enough to even begin tonight."

Joanna, suddenly aware of time passing, pulled away. "We should go back to the gym."

"I suppose so," Pete agreed reluctantly.

"I can't go back looking like this. I left my purse inside, but I have a cosmetic bag in my car. And there's an extra key under the front bumper."

"You've taken on big city ways, my love. We don't lock our cars in Greenville," he teased as he followed her to the front of the Honda, knelt down, and retrieved the key. He opened the door, then wrapped his arms around her and whispered against her hair, "Joanna, when will I see you again?"

"I don't know." She hadn't thought beyond tonight, beyond this first meeting.

"I don't intend to lose you this time," he said, pulling her close. He bent to meet her lips with another searing kiss that left them both shaken. He waited as she sat down, opened a small clutch bag, and by the light of the visor mirror repaired her makeup.

"Watching you now reminds me of other times and places when you did this before I took you home after a date," Pete said wistfully.

Joanna shook her head as though to banish the image Pete's words had evoked. "My father always waited up for me."

Pete nodded, said in a grim tone, "I well remember."

Reluctantly, they returned to the gym and joined the crowd on the dance floor. The band had been instructed to play Elvis and of course, they did. Joanna and Pete walked in to his voice filling the gym. Meeting Pete's eyes again in the dim light, she smiled and his arm tightened possessively.

"Hey, it's my turn to dance with Joanna." Al tapped Pete's shoulder and he released her to their classmate's open arms. "I've stepped on Vada's toes until she had to sit this one out."

Joanna laughed as she adjusted her steps to follow Al's lead. Boyd and Betsy glided by just then and Boyd winked at her as Betsy wiggled the fingers of one hand on Boyd's shoulder in greeting.

"It's great to see you two together again. Just like old times." Al grinned at her.

Joanna smiled. "And now it is we who are getting older."

"Only as old as we feel, kid, and I'm feeling younger by the minute." He laughed. "Maybe it's too much beer. Seriously, we hope you'll stick around awhile. Pete's not been getting out much since...hell, it seems awkward talking about her to you, since you and Pete, what I mean is..."

"It's okay, Al," Joanna assured him when he seemed unable to finish. "I'm glad I came. It's so good to see all of you, and I promise I'll see more of you." Now why did she say that? She wasn't at all sure that was true. At least, she hadn't thought about it until now but it sounded like a good idea.

Pete and Thelma circled by them and returned. "Al, Vada says she's ready for something to drink," Thelma called to him. "And Joanna, you can have Pete back. He's too good for me. I'd swear he's been taking dance lessons."

Pete laughed as he took Joanna in his arms without missing a step. Thelma turned and followed Al toward their table.

"Should we join the others?" Joanna asked.

"Not yet. Just one more dance and then we will."

Pete led her in a slow circle to the other side of the room and paused beside the wishing well, feet staying in one place, as their bodies rocked in time with the music.

"Remember this, Joanna? It's prom night all over again."

"I remember."

"And we made a wish and tossed pennies into the well. And then we danced around behind it where the chaperones couldn't see us and sealed our wishes with a stolen kiss."

Joanna laughed softly. "But Vada and Al caught us."

"Yeah, they were hiding, too." Suddenly sounding serious, Pete asked, "Did your wish come true, Joanna?"

Joanna shook her head, unable to speak.

"Neither did mine, but maybe it's not too late."

She looked at his handsome face in the shadows which erased the visible lines of time. And saw the boy she loved. For a moment she almost believed the meaning behind his words. Then with a sudden sharp clarity, she remembered why it could never be.

"Want to make our wishes again, just to be certain?" Pete whispered.

Joanna shook her head with regret. "No, Pete.

We can't wish over."

She closed her eyes, feeling the rhythm of the music and the familiar nearness of the boy who became a man, the remembered yesterdays merging with the unreality of this night. She was glad, so glad that she had come back. She had opened the door to the past and there could be no future, but tonight was hers to treasure forever.

Too soon, the band played their final number and began packing up their instruments as Thelma, Vada, and Bets congratulated themselves and Pete on a job well done. Joanna's classmates were slow to take leave of her and only did so after she promised to see them again soon. Pete lingered a few moments more, his eyes caressing her, then with reluctance said goodnight when Betsy announced that they should be going.

Joanna kept Betsy's pickup truck in sight as she drove the dark road. It was hard to believe Pete Damron had walked back into her life and awakened emotions she had forgotten existed. Even now, her lips were still tingling from his kisses and her whole body was alive with sensations that made her feel seventeen again.

Seventeen and on the way to Betsy's house after a night of fun with Pete and all the gang. Pete driving his dad's old Ford pickup with her scrunched between him and Bets in spite of the awkward gear shift. And stealing a last goodnight kiss as he walked them to the door. She had always begged permission to stay over with Bets after school activities because going home to face the inquisition of her father had taken the joy out of her good time. Betsy's mom had greeted them with cocoa and cookies and listened as they regaled her with the night's happenings while she smiled her approval.

Up ahead, she saw Betsy's truck slow and then turn into the familiar driveway. Bets had told her how she and Walt had stayed on the farm and taken care of her mom after they were married. For a moment, she wondered what it would be like to live in a place like this again but quickly pushed the thought from her mind.

****

Joanna had changed into white satin pajamas while Betsy made cocoa and the two of them were now comfortably ensconced at opposite ends of the well-worn den sofa.

"Mmmmmm, delicious." Joanna tasted the steaming liquid, then held her cup in both hands. "And marshmallows, just like your mom used to make for us."

Betsy nodded. "Only this comes from a store packet."

"It still tastes the same." Joanna smiled at her. "And takes me right back to all those sleepovers when we stayed awake half the night."

"Ah, those were the days. Not like later when I was staying awake with crying babies."

After a small silence, Joanna shook her head. "One minute we were girls, and now you have all those children older than we were then."

"And you have a great career. There's a lot to be said for the single life." She clapped her hands over her mouth, then added, "Pretend I didn't say that. We're all hoping that you and Pete, well, if you're not serious about anyone else..."

Joanna shook her head. "No, there's never been anyone else. I just haven't found another Pete, I guess."

"He didn't find another Joanna either. Oh, he and Mary Esther had a good marriage, I think. But he never looked at her the way he used to look at you, the way he looked at you tonight."

"I guess first love is special. At least, it was for me."

"I don't think Pete would ever have married anyone else if Mary Esther hadn't thrown herself at him when he came home on leave. She was determined to have him. You weren't around and he seemed different somehow." She sighed. "I've often wondered what it would have been like to have you just down the road all these years instead of Mary Esther. I've missed you, Joanna."

"And I've missed you, Bets." She put down her empty cup and tucked her feet up. "It wasn't that I wanted to lose touch or never come back. It was just that I couldn't have it both ways. After Pete and I, well, I had to make a clean break."

"I understand that now. But for a long time I felt you had rejected me, your best friend."

"No, Betsy, never."

"When your parents came back for the dedication of the new sanctuary in the Methodist Church, I went, hoping you'd be with them. But your mother said you were at Lambuth and she'd ask you to write, but you never did."

"I guess she forgot to tell me." She was certain her father had forbidden her mother to do so but it didn't matter now. She reached for Betsy's hand. "Now I'm back, I promise to make up for lost time." Why was she promising to do that when this was supposed to be a one-time fling to rid herself of all those memories that refused to go away?

Betsy stifled a yawn as she stood. "I've been awake since four this morning, and I'm beat so we'd better continue this tomorrow. What time would you like to have breakfast?"

"A little later than four, if you don't mind," Joanna answered with a wry smile and they both burst into giggles. She gathered their empty mugs and rinsed them in the sink while Betsy turned off the downstairs lights.

At the top of the steps, Betsy hugged her

affectionately. "Good night, Joanna. Sleep well."

"Good night, Bets. Thanks so much for asking me to stay."

"Oh, I almost forgot. I invited Pete to have lunch with us tomorrow. I hope you don't mind?"

"Of course not," Joanna assured her.

"I haven't seen him looking so happy since I don't know when."

As Joanna lay in bed she thought of Betsy's words about Pete and Mary Esther. She didn't like the thought of another girl determined to become Mrs. Peter Damron. Another woman as Pete's wife, having his children, being Betsy's neighbor.

His children! Pete had said he wanted her to meet them but she hadn't done so. Perhaps he'd had other things on his mind besides his family. But there would be other times. No, she cautioned herself. She wouldn't think of the future for now. Betsy had asked Pete to come for lunch tomorrow and things would no doubt look very different in the light of day than in the shadows of this nostalgic night. Unaccustomed to the quiet darkness, it was a long while before Joanna fell asleep to dream of Pete.

CHAPTER THREE

Joanna awoke with bright sunlight shining in her eyes, disoriented by her unfamiliar surroundings; then remembered her impulsive decision last night.

Betsy was in the downstairs kitchen but it smelled the same as it had on other Sunday mornings when she had slept over. Mass! What time was it?

After splashing her face with cold water and brushing her hair, Joanna joined Betsy in the kitchen. "Good morning, Bets. Why didn't you wake me when you got up?"

Betsy looked up from the griddle she was attending and smiled. "I was just about to call you. Thought I'd finish the bacon and fix the French toast first."

"French toast? Like your mother used to make for us?" Betsy nodded, then she asked, "Won't you be late for Mass?"

Betsy shook her head. "I stopped going after the twins left home. God didn't seem to be there anymore, at least not for me."

"I stopped going to church, too." Joanna sat down at the table where two floral place mats and pastel stoneware plates had been set.

"What would your father say to that?" Betsy asked in a low voice as she placed the bacon on a small platter and dipped thick pieces of bread in batter.

"That I'll burn in hell." Joanna smiled wryly. "But he'd already threatened that, long ago."

Betsy looked expectant but Joanna, lost in thought, did not go on. After a moment, Betsy spoke. "There's orange juice in the fridge. And coffee's perked if you'd like a cup now."

Coming abruptly back to the present, Joanna stood, and went to the counter where the coffee maker sat. "Coffee is definitely in order."

After breakfast and third cups of coffee, the two women made quick work of loading the dishwasher and went out to Betsy's garden. The morning sun felt good on Joanna's pale skin and she reveled in the feel of leafy vines wet with dew and the smell of rich dirt and compost.

"What a treat," Joanna said as they brought baskets from the garden. "English peas right off the vine. I'd almost forgotten where they came from."

"Fat chance I'd forget," Betsy laughed, "considering all the work it takes to grow them." She set her basket down in front of the garage adjacent to the house.

Joanna's eye caught sight of a bicycle leaning against the wall beside Betsy's blue truck. "Do you still ride a bike, Bets?"

"Gosh, no. There's two or three still around here, though. The twins ride them when they come home."

Joanna walked over to the nearest bike, tentatively took hold of its rusted handle bars. "It's been years since I rode one, too. But it used to be such fun." Joanna pushed the bike out of the garage. "Let's go for a ride now, Betsy. Just a short one, for old time's sake."

Betsy shrugged. "Why not? If I can remember how." She went into the garage and came out pushing a dilapidated blue bike.

"They say you never forget how to ride a bicycle." Joanna smiled encouragingly.

"Well, we can prove that one way or the other, can't we?" Betsy asked as she warily eyed the bike. "Want to ride this one? It's the only girl's bike here."

"No, I'm taller. I'll have an easier time than you on this one." Joanna lifted a leg over the crossbar, planted one foot on a pedal, and gave a push with the other. Getting her balance, she pumped with uncertain legs at first, then feeling confident, headed for the road. "Come on, Bets, it's still fun."

"I'm coming, Joanna." Betsy followed at a slower pace at first, then gained momentum as the spring wind pushed her from behind.

Joanna felt the sun on her back and the wind in her hair and knew a moment of pure pleasure unlike any she had experienced in a very long time. She glanced behind her, saw Betsy laboring to keep up, and called back to her. "Want to turn back?"

"Not yet." Betsy pulled beside her, then added. "Pete's place is just beyond that clump of trees."

"I didn't realize..." Joanna faltered. "It was dark last night and I wasn't paying attention."

"He has his father's land now, as well as the farm that he and—the farm he bought next to it when he came back to Greenville. But the house is only a few years old. He built it on the same shady site as the smaller one where he raised his family. You can't see it very well since it's so far back from the road but it's really nice and—"

Joanna, attention focused on the brick ranch-style house half hidden by the pale green foliage of new-leafed maples, did not see the broken pavement that caused her bike to lurch and then careen out of control. Because of the crossbar, she was unable to jump clear when the bicycle overturned leaving her tangled under its heavy weight.

"Joanna, oh my God, are you hurt?" Betsy

braked to a sudden stop just ahead of her and came running.

"No." Joanna winced at the pain in her foot as she tried to move and amended uncertainly, "I don't know." As Betsy peered anxiously above her, she added, "But maybe if you can get this monster off me, I could..."

"Of course. Can you move your other leg without hurting?" When Joanna complied, Betsy gingerly lifted the bike, then knelt to assess her friend's injuries. "You've scraped the whole side of your leg on the asphalt, looks like, and it's bleeding on your white slacks. Do you think you could make it to Pete's house if I help you?"

"Oh, no, Betsy. We can't go there. Besides, he's probably at Mass."

"Nope, truck's in the driveway. And you can't walk all the way back to my house like that." She looked at the offending bike. "And you certainly can't ride. Come on, I'll help you."

Joanna made an attempt to stand and the sharp pain in her right foot caused her to sit down on the pavement again. "I—I think I may have sprained my ankle, Bets."

"Or it could be broken." Betsy looked concerned. "You just sit there and don't move. I'll get Pete and we'll be right back."

Before Joanna could protest, Betsy had mounted her bike and was headed toward Pete's house. *What a mess I've made of things,* Joanna wailed silently. Pete was coming to lunch and she had hoped to put her best foot forward and here she was sprawled all over the road looking like an awkward fool.

She heard a motor start, and saw Pete's truck coming rapidly toward her. With a screech of brakes, he came to a halt on the road beside her and jumped out, Betsy following.

Feeling vulnerable as she sat there on the

pavement, Joanna's heart gave a sudden leap of happiness at the sight of him. Mustering a wry smile, she shrugged.

"Hello, Pete. Thanks for coming to my rescue."

"Hello, Joanna. Looks like you've had quite a fall there."

He knelt and gently touched her foot and she winced. "Hurt?"

When she nodded, he examined it closer and frowned. "It's swelling already."

He took the offending foot in both hands, tentatively probed as he questioned the degree of pain with each movement. "Doesn't appear to be broken, but it's a bad sprain."

He caressed her foot, the feel of his work-roughened hands sharply contrasting with her soft skin. The touch of his gentle fingers on her throbbing ankle suffused her body with a wave of longing to be held and comforted until the pain went away. Surely she must be dreaming. It was not possible that she, Joanna Flemming, was sitting here in the bright sunlight of a Sunday morning while Pete Damron sent shivers of desire coursing through her like electric shock waves.

"Pete," she whispered, as he cleared his throat and spoke simultaneously.

"We'd better get you to the house." He put a hand under her arm, lifted her carefully. "Just lean on me, don't put any weight on that foot now."

He guided her slowly to the truck, helped her in, while Betsy picked up the fallen bicycle.

"I need to see to lunch," Betsy told them. "If you can take care of Joanna, I'll just ride on home. Then you two can come later."

"Sure, Bets," Pete agreed quickly. "And I'll bring the other bike in the truck."

"Twelve o'clock. Don't be late," Betsy said as Pete went around to the other side of the cab. "Way to go," she added softly to Joanna. "I hoped Pete would notice us and this sure got his attention in a hurry."

"I didn't do it on purpose," Joanna whispered, horrified.

"I know," Bets whispered back and giggled. "God moves in mysterious ways."

"I thought you didn't believe God was here anymore?" Joanna was starting to smile as she teased Bets.

"He's not in church. But He is out here." Bets raised an eyebrow as Pete slammed the driver's door. She winked at Joanna and rode away, a satisfied smile on her face.

Later, leaning into Pete's solid support, Joanna limped to the leather sofa and sat down, careful not to brush her blood-stained slacks against the cushions.

"I'll get First Aid supplies and be right back," Pete assured her. "Make yourself at home."

Home. Joanna looked around her. This house could have been her home if only she and Pete...She concentrated on the furnishings, large comfortable pieces suited to a man. The nearest wall was entirely lined with bookshelves, crowded with well-worn books, and on the table beside her two volumes lay. Walt Whitman and Thoreau. It surprised her that Pete would read poetry.

"All set." Pete grinned at Joanna as he came to kneel before her. "Surgery is about to begin." He pushed the leg of her slacks higher, dipped white gauze in a small basin, and cleansed her wounds. "This will sting," he cautioned as he dabbed antiseptic on the raw abrasions.

Joanna bit her lip to keep from crying out and Pete cupped her face in his hands. "I don't like hurting you," he said softly. He covered her mouth with his and kissed her. Pulling back finally, he said in a half-jesting voice, "I like playing doctor with you, but I'm sorry I'm having all the pleasure and you the pain." Joanna smiled in answer and after a moment he continued, "I'll bandage this and then we'll see about getting the blood off your clothes."

He taped clean gauze over the scraped skin, wound elastic around her ankle for support, and tried ineffectively to remove the dark red spots. "Won't this stain if it dries?" he asked.

Joanna nodded. "Probably, unless it's soaked in cold water."

"Then you'd better take off your slacks and let me put them in the tub." He stood up. "I'll get you something else to wear."

Starting to protest, Joanna thought of her expensive new slacks and remained quiet. She steeled herself for an offered garment of Mary Esther's, probably something small that she couldn't even get into. But when Pete returned, he was carrying a white terry wrap-around robe.

"Here, put this on while I make coffee." He handed it to her and turned away as she gratefully shrugged out of her slacks.

Later, as her slacks soaked and they sipped coffee, Joanna said, "You have a nice house, Pete."

"Thanks. I'd show you the other rooms but it wouldn't help your foot to walk anymore than you have to."

"I see you have a swimming pool." She looked toward the back of the house, where blue water glinted in the sunlight beyond the glass sliding doors.

"Yeah. It's been a lot of work but the kids love it. And now the grandchildren are enjoying it."

Joanna swallowed past a lump in her throat. It was hard to think of Pete with children and a wife. And now the children of Pete's children frolicked here. If only—

"Do you still swim?" Pete's words cut into her thoughts.

"When I have time. And speaking of time, shouldn't we be getting back to Betsy's house soon?"

"Right. I'll just put your slacks in the dryer for a few minutes and we'll be on our way." He stood up. "Low heat, delicate cycle?"

She nodded, smiled. "I'm impressed."

"One learns how to do laundry," Pete shrugged, "after wearing pink underwear that's two sizes too small."

Joanna laughed aloud as Pete disappeared through the door. The sound of her own laughter startled her. How long had it been since she had really laughed? She was actually having fun in spite of all her reservations about coming and her ridiculous accident.

Lost in thoughts of Pete, she was startled to find him standing before her, slacks held between them. He knelt and pulled them over her feet, then said, "Better let me help you up, then hold onto to my shoulders while I fasten them."

"I'm sure that I—" she began, but he was lifting her and her arms went around his neck without further protest. His hands slid the slacks to her waist, fumbled inexpertly with the fastener, and her heart pounded as she felt the warmth of his fingers against her bare skin. "Pete, I can—"

His hand suddenly moved to the small of her back and he pulled her closer and buried her head against his shoulder. "Oh, Joanna, Joanna, when I touch you this way..."

She raised her head, met his eager lips, welcomed the passion of his probing tongue. When the evidence of his wanting pressed against her, she fought her own desire to match his urgency and said breathlessly, "Pete, please, we have to go. Betsy will be waiting."

With a resigned groan, he took a step backward, being careful to support her still. "If Betsy wasn't such a good friend, I'd say to hell with lunch and we'd satisfy a hunger for more than food today."

"There will be other times, Pete," she whispered.

"Promise?"

"Promise." There, she'd committed herself. Only what if she had second thoughts when she had time to think about it? A chill clutched her heart. Or what if he did?

****

Back at Beekman Place late Sunday evening, Joanna balanced her weight on the unfamiliar crutches and searched her handbag for the door key. She wished she'd had the foresight to leave it in her pocket.

"Joanna?" A door opened down the hall and a petite woman came toward her. Eve Whitfield was new to Memphis State this year and things had not been the same since she arrived. The former hippie with her long braided titian hair, floral skirts, and brightly woven serapes was a sharp contrast to the more sedate faculty members.

Joanna turned to greet her next door neighbor with an air of studied nonchalance. "Hello, Eve."

"I heard all the bumping out here and I—what on earth happened to you?" She reached Joanna just in time to grab one falling crutch as the door swung open. "Here, you go on in, I'll get your bag."

Inside, Eve set the luggage on the floor and stood surveying Joanna who had collapsed into the nearest chair. "That must have been some reunion."

"I fell off a bike," Joanna explained.

"A bike?" Eve's face lit up with excitement. "They rode bikes at the reunion? What a unique idea."

"No, I rode with an old friend this morning." Seeing from her neighbor's expression more was expected, she added, "The one I spent the night with."

Eve's eyebrows shot up. "*The* old friend?"

"No, if you mean what I think—" Joanna hastily corrected the misconception and continued, "I sprained my ankle."

"Did you get it x-rayed or anything?"

"No, but Pete examined it."

"Pete? Aha, the plot thickens."

Joanna had confided to Eve her misgivings about returning to Greenville and seeing Pete after all these years so it was no surprise her curiosity was piqued at mention of his name.

"We were riding near his house when I fell, so he took care of me."

"Sweet. And the reunion, was it all you expected?" Eve looked at her intently.

"Yes, it was lovely. I'm so glad I went."

"This I've got to hear. You come home late looking exhausted, hobbling on crutches after practically killing yourself, and tell me it was lovely. Let me make tea and put your things away, and you can tell me all about it."

Joanna resigned herself to giving Eve a detailed account of the weekend in Greenville even though her ankle was throbbing from the long drive home. After all, without Eve's encouragement she might have turned down the invitation to the reunion and missed seeing Pete again. But would she regret taking this step back into the past? The first misgivings about what she had done nibbled at the edges of her mind and she made a conscious effort to ignore them.

Eve insisted on taking care of her so she graciously accepted the food and fellowship her good neighbor provided. To expedite faster healing of her ankle, Joanna spent most of the following day on a sofa with her foot propped up. She attempted to use the time working on plans for summer classes but thoughts of Pete Damron kept intruding. Finally she gave up any attempt to work and sat staring at the TV screen while her mind replayed every detail of the past weekend in Greenville.

"Time to feed you," Eve's voice interrupted her reverie as she let herself in the door.

"You really don't need to do this," Joanna protested mildly as Eve served her dinner on a TV tray.

"Shush, there is no reason for you to hobble around on a painful foot when—"

The phone interrupted her words and at Joanna's nod she went to the kitchen to answer. A moment later, she was back carrying the cordless receiver.

"It's a man," she said softly. "He didn't say who."

Joanna immediately thought of Pete and tried to keep her voice casual. "Hello?"

"Joanna, this is Pete. How are you?"

"Still limping a bit but otherwise I'm fine."

"Since you have someone there, would you like me to call back later?"

"No," she answered quickly. "This is fine. My next-door neighbor brought dinner for me." *And she was just leaving,* she added hopefully to herself. But Eve seemed to be in no hurry to do that, rearranging the dishes on the tray, humming softly.

"I, uh, I wanted to follow up on what you promised yesterday. That is, if you haven't changed your mind."

"No, I...no." It was very awkward carrying on this conversation with Eve listening to every word. She had sat down and picked up a magazine, peeking over the pages expectantly at Joanna.

"I have business in Memphis this week, and I'd like to see you."

"That will be...fine. What day?"

"Friday, if it's not a bad time for you?"

"No, I mean yes, it's fine."

"Then I'd like to take you to dinner. Would six be too early?"

"Six is fine." Eve raised her eyebrows again as Joanna gave Pete directions to the condo and then said goodbye.

"The old friend?" Joanna nodded and Eve looked pleased. "And he's coming here to see you which I gather from all those replies you gave him is *fine* with you."

"He's coming here on business, and he invited me to dinner."

"Great." Eve seemed momentarily uncertain. "At least, I think it is. I'll mention it to Marvella and let you know."

"Don't you dare." Joanna picked up her fork and speared a piece of beef with a vigorous jab. "I don't need a fortune teller's approval to have dinner with an old friend." She didn't want anyone predicting what would happen between her and Pete this time around.

"Mmmm, you're right." Eve brightened. "I'll just do a Zodiac chart on him. That should be enough for now."

"Not without his birth date you won't," Joanna said smugly. "And I'm not telling." Her renewed relationship with Pete was far too fragile to be dissected by astrological charts. She didn't want to know their future yet.

"You mean you dated him without knowing his sign?" Eve asked in a shocked voice. "That's probably why you split up to begin with, incompatible. Well, you'll just have to find out right away. No point in wasting your time on something that's not in the stars."

"True," she agreed to all of Eve's observations with one word, then determinedly changed the subject. “This stroganoff is delicious.” Joanna smiled at Eve as she stood up to leave. “And it was really very thoughtful of you to bring dinner tonight.”

“No problem.” Eve accepted the gratitude with a deprecating wave. “It satisfied my need to feel maternal.”

Joanna watched Eve let herself out the door, then her thoughts returned to Peter Damron and yesterday. She wondered where their passionate kisses would have led if Betsy hadn’t been expecting them to lunch. In her condo there would be no schedules to keep. What if Pete wanted...what if she wanted...there was still time to stop what was happening between them. But did she really want to? It was something she would have to decide before Friday. She hadn’t felt this way about a date since high school when she had waited for Pete in her parents’ living room at the parsonage. How long ago that seemed. That he still had the power to evoke such adolescent feelings surprised her. She had a premonition that if she gave herself completely to Peter Damron again she would lose control of all her ability to reason and that was scary.

CHAPTER FOUR

As the Memphis City Limits sign came in view, Pete adjusted the cruise control and glanced at his watch. Only two hours and twenty minutes had separated him from Joanna all this time but it might as well have been a million light years.

He went first to the farm machinery dealer and made fast work of selecting a new tractor and arranging delivery. He could have made the purchase in St. Louis as usual but this had given him a legitimate reason for being in town.

Following Joanna's explicit directions, he thought of their first meeting again. He had prepared his speech and practiced it aloud, committing it to memory. "Hello Joanna. It's been a long time. How have you been?" But in spite of his careful preparation, he'd acted like a lovesick kid, blurting out how she was as pretty as ever.

He'd left the building and stood alone in the darkness to get his emotions under control. And to stop acting like a damned idiot. Because she *was* as pretty as she had been at seventeen, with her thick dark hair, big brown eyes and full lips that were made for kissing. And in that white dress that fit her in all the right places he saw that she was no longer a winsome girl but a very desirable woman.

She seemed as receptive to his ardor as she always was when he kissed her. It was impossible for them to have enough time together to explore the years they'd been apart when all of their classmates expected to spend time with Joanna, too. And the next day they had been dictated by Betsy's plans for lunch. But he wouldn't fault her for that. If not for Bets, Joanna might have gone back to Memphis after the reunion, making it more difficult for him to follow up on their first meeting.

Using the code Joanna had supplied, he entered the gated complex and found visitor's parking. The five-story brick building with tall columns bespoke simple affluence which was echoed inside by the potted palms lining the marble-tiled hallway. Pete pressed the elevator button and selected the fifth floor. He scarcely had time to straighten his jacket and adjust his tie before he found himself walking toward Joanna's door, his footsteps silent on the plush carpet.

He rang the bell as he ran one finger inside his shirt collar which seemed to be cutting off his breath. The door opened and there she stood, her beauty leaving him awe-struck anew. He swallowed and mustered a smile.

"Hello, Pete, come in." She moved aside for him to enter but he stood for a moment just looking at her.

It was Joanna, of course, but not the girl he knew, nor even the woman who had bedazzled him last weekend when she came back to Greenville. This was a sophisticated college professor, a high rise dweller who stood before him in her black fitted dress and expensive-looking gold jewelry. For a moment, he couldn't find his voice and when the words came they sounded unfamiliar to his ears. "Joanna, how...elegant you look."

"Thank you." She smiled. "You look nice, too."

He was wearing the suit he had bought for the reunion but his shirt and tie were new for this occasion.

"How have you been?"

"I'm mending nicely, thanks to a good man with a First Aid kit." She repeated "Come in," reached out, touched his arm, drew him inside. "I'll get my jacket."

Pete's eyes swept the room, conscious of its understated but pricey decor, its precise placement of furniture and accessories. It was nothing like the parsonage where he'd come for Joanna yet it made him decidedly more uncomfortable, even without the imposing presence of the Reverend Flemming.

"Nice place," he said politely, thinking his tone probably betrayed how ill at ease he felt. Joanna held out a teal silk jacket and he helped her into it.

As she turned to lock the door, a voice spoke behind her. "Well, hello, Joanna. Going out, I see."

The woman, dressed in purple sweats, stood waiting expectantly, eyes on Peter Damron in keen appraisal.

"Why, Eve, how nice that you came by just now. You can meet my old friend, Peter Damron."

"Helloooo," Eve cooed, extending her hand as she looked up into Pete's face which was considerably above her own.

"Pete, this is Eve Whitfield, my next door neighbor who has fed me all week."

He took her hand. "Hello, nice to meet you, Eve."

"You, too, Pete. Joanna has told me about your beautiful farm."

"Yes, well, thanks." Pete looked even more uncomfortable than before as he carefully withdrew his hand from her grip.

"Modest, prudent. You're a Capricorn, right?"

"What?"

"Capricorn. Your zodiac sign."

"Oh, I'm afraid I don't pay much attention to astrology."

"Your birthday is in January, right?" Eve persisted.

"Why, yes. The eighth."

"Wonderful." Eve gave Joanna a triumphant look. "Nice meeting you. I'll be going now, I've some charting to do. You two have a lovely dinner."

With a sigh, Joanna turned back to Pete. "Eve is a great believer in astrological predictions. I'm afraid before the weekend is over, I'll be hearing whether your sign and mine are compatible and probably what her psychic friend Marvella thinks about it."

Pete grinned at her. "Well, I hope the stars are in my favor, if it means anything to you."

Joanna shook her head. "I'm a skeptic myself."

He laughed and changed the subject. "Any place special you'd like to go for dinner?" he asked as they rode down the elevator. "I'd like you to choose."

"Well, there's a restaurant out by the airport that serves good food and they have a lounge that plays a lot of Elvis music. I go there sometimes."

"Sounds fine to me." Pete took Joanna's arm as they reached the ground floor and guided her across the lobby. Elvis music and dancing. Things were looking up after all.

The restaurant was filled with locals celebrating the end of another work week and they had to wait for a table. Pete noticed that Joanna was still walking with a slight limp in spite of her low-heeled shoes. He realized belatedly that he should have made a reservation somewhere ahead of time.

"Want to have a drink while we wait?" Pete motioned toward the lounge, then suddenly seemed about to withdraw the invitation. "That is, if you, I mean—" Why hadn't he remembered that she was a minister's daughter and probably still abided by her Holy Father's commandment never to taste alcohol?

"A drink would be fine."

He led the way into the smoke-filled room and

found a small table.

"I'll have a pina colada," she told the cocktail waitress who took their order. "Frozen."

"Whiskey sour," Pete added.

"Doctor Flemming, hello." A slender blond girl at another table was waving in their direction and he turned to look at Joanna who was waving back.

"Still at the university?" the girl called again. Joanna nodded. "And you, Debbie?"

"Married, a baby. Parents' night out." She got up to dance with a tall man who nodded to them as he held her chair. Then seeming to change her mind, she came toward their table. "I'd like you to meet my husband, Mike. This is Dr. Flemming, my English prof." She laughed. "The one I was always complaining about being such a slave driver. And this is...?" She looked at Pete with frank curiosity and paused.

"Peter Damron," Joanna supplied, and added, "an old school friend of mine."

Pete rose to take the girl's proffered hand and then shook hands with the man beside her.

"College classmate or faculty?" Debbie asked.

"No, I—" Pete began but Joanna cut in smoothly.

"Pete and I went to high school together."

"Oh." Debbie looked chagrined but quickly recovered and smiled at Pete. "Nice meeting you, Mister Damron." She took her husband's arm and turned back with a wink at Pete. "She's the greatest." She waved to them both."Good to see you again, Doctor Flemming. Bye now. Have a wonderful evening."

"One of my favorite students," Joanna said, still looking at the couple as they walked toward the crowded dance floor.

"So I gathered," Pete said quietly, then asked, "Does everyone refer to you that way?"

Joanna frowned. "What way?"

"As *Doctor* Flemming?"

Joanna laughed. "Oh, I thought for a minute you meant as a slave driver." She shook her head. "No, only the kids I teach and some of my colleagues."

Pete attempted to make light of his question. "Good, then I can still call you Joanna."

Their drinks arrived and Joanna took the frosted glass and sipped the frothy pink concoction slowly as Pete took one hefty slug of his drink, then sat swirling the remaining liquid with studied concentration. He hoped the dining room would call their names soon, because an awkward silence hung between them now, and he could think of nothing to say.

To his relief, the wait was short. But as the hostess led them to their table, a middle-aged couple stepped in front of them.

"Doctor Flemming, how nice to see you," the stylish woman said and lightly touched her arm.

"What a pleasant surprise," her balding companion added. "Where have you been keeping yourself?"

"Oh, I've been quite busy of late," Joanna said with a meaningful look at Pete.

"Congratulations on getting your article published in *The English Journal*," the woman smiled sincerely. "The faculty is all abuzz about it, you know."

"Thank you." The couple stood blocking their path to the vacant table and Joanna turned to Pete. "I'd like you to meet two of my colleagues, Doctors Jane and Rudolph Meir. Pete Damron, an old friend of mine."

"Hello, Doctor Damron," Jane Meir said and extended her heavily ringed hand.

"I'm not—" Pete began but Joanna cut in quickly. "Pete is from Missouri where I grew up."

"Pleasure to meet you," Rudolph Meir said and pumped Pete's hand vigorously. "Why don't you join us at our faculty brunch in the morning? Any guest of Doctor Flemming would be very welcome." He turned to Joanna and added, "You will be coming, won't you? Everyone is eager to hear about your coup getting accepted by the top notch journal in your field."

"I—well, I'm not certain." She gestured toward the hostess who stood waiting. "I think we'd better claim our table before someone else does. Nice to see you both."

Ordering diverted their attention for an interval and then Pete looked at Joanna and smiled. "It seems congratulations are in order here. Why didn't you tell me?"

Joanna shrugged. "I guess it would have seemed like bragging."

"Not to me. I'm very proud for you. Have you been published before?"

"A couple of times." She smiled and shrugged again. "It's publish or perish, you know."

"No," Pete looked at her apologetically. "I didn't know."

"Well, enough about me," she said decisively. "Tell me what you bought today."

As their meal progressed and talk turned to earlier times and friends, the mood of the evening lightened. When they had finished second cups of coffee, the vibes between them were almost visible in their intensity.

"Would you like to order dessert now?" Pete asked Joanna as the waiter cleared their plates.

"No, thank you, but they have wonderful chocolate pies."

"I think I'll pass, too." Pete addressed the waiter, "May we have our check, please?"

She glanced at her watch. "It's almost time for

the show."

Pete held her chair, then took her arm and led her through the crowded room to a table near the dance floor. He repeated their earlier drink orders just as the band appeared on stage and the music began.

The singer crooned a familiar tune and Pete and Joanna wordlessly rose and began moving to the music.

It felt right to have Joanna in his arms again, Pete thought. He closed his eyes, transported back in time to Greenville, Yokely's Drug Store and the juke box blaring out the same song.

"Who said 'The more things change, the more they stay the same'?" she asked in a low voice and he knew her memories were identical.

"I don't know," he whispered back, "but it seems true, doesn't it?"

"It does right now," she answered, as he pulled her closer so that her breath was warm against his face.

Their bodies were communicating in a language only lovers speak and they fell silent and listened. The song ended and the band's tempo speeded up.

Pete looked at Joanna. "Feel like sitting this one out?"

"Definitely."

They returned to their table, sipped their drinks, and watched the dancers. Then Pete turned his attention to Joanna, studying her face in profile. It was easy to ignore the gulf between them, to go back in time. Touching her, holding her, he could almost forget that Mary Esther had ever been his wife and finally left him with an empty heart. But it wasn't empty, had never been. There was always Joanna, only he hadn't admitted that until now.

Another slow song began, and he reached for her hand. She looked at him, smiled tremulously, and he felt himself grow hot with desire. Did she feel this hormonal surge of pure sexual need, too? Well, there was only one way to find out.

"Are you ready, Joanna?" He didn't say ready to go, ready to make love, just left the rest of the sentence for her to finish.

She nodded, and he rose and pulled out her chair. His hand lightly resting on her arm sent vibrations to every nerve ending in his whole body as they made their way toward the parking lot. He felt alive, so alive it was almost painful to breathe.

On the drive back, they held hands, saying little as if both feared breaking the magic spell that encompassed them. At her place, Joanna directed Pete to the parking area designated for overnight guest parking. The elevator seemed to be interminably slow, and she fumbled with her key.

After an awkward moment inside, she said, "I'll make coffee." She glanced toward the stereo as she passed it, but switched on the TV instead. "Make yourself comfortable. The news should be on in a second."

Pete removed his jacket, and sat down on one of the twin sofas. The news. Coffee. Was Joanna stalling for time? Had he misread her cues? He felt beads of sweat form on the back of his neck and opened his shirt collar. The local newscaster greeted him from the wide screen and he turned away and went into Joanna's kitchen. It was all white, as sterile and almost as bare as an operating room.

"Coffee's ready." She poured two cups, set them on a tray which he carried to the living room. They drank in silence, watching the changing images on the TV screen.

It was time to make his move. Take Joanna in his arms and show her how much he wanted her. But here in this unfamiliar room she seemed so...untouchable. Not like in the dim-lit lounge a while ago when memories had obscured the woman she had become.

"I really ought to be going. It's a long drive to Greenville and we farmers are not used to late hours." He smiled apologetically.

"Oh? I thought maybe you were staying over," Joanna answered in a barely audible voice.

He put down his cup, stood. "Thanks for the coffee. And the evening."

She gave him his coat. "Thank you for asking me, Pete." She followed him to the door. "I had a lovely time."

He turned toward her, hesitated, then kissed her in an oddly impersonal way.

"Drive carefully." Joanna closed the door softly behind him and he heard the sound of the dead bolt as he walked toward the elevator.

Pete was driving too fast after he crossed the bridge, and he set the cruise control on the speed limit, and forced himself to try and relax. He had to figure out what happened back there. He'd wanted Joanna and he was certain she felt the same about him. But when they'd returned to her place, he had suddenly seen her as she was, not as the memory she evoked in that smoky lounge. And Joanna-the-woman was someone he didn't even know, much less love. Or want to make love to. There, in her own setting, she had not even seemed approachable.

He was already wondering what a woman like Joanna could possible see in a Missouri cotton farmer and now he felt even more certain that the answer was nothing. Nothing at all. He could never fit in attending faculty functions as Doctor Flemming's husband. He understood now that there was more separating them than a couple of hours travel and a lot of silent years. It wasn't going to work between him and Joanna so he'd go home to grow cotton and let Doctor Flemming get on with her life at the university.

He resigned himself to the obvious as the car moved monotonously through the darkness toward its destination.

CHAPTER FIVE

Joanna finished grading the last theme paper from a stack on her wicker tray, put down her felt-tip marker, and removed her reading glasses. She replaced the tray with her crocheted afghan and let her mind wander to Pete. It had been almost a month and she hadn't heard from him since he had chastely kissed her goodnight after their dinner date. She could have called him, but doubt held her back. Maybe he'd realized that it was a mistake to try and resurrect the past, cut his losses and run. Still, she wished—the phone rang and she glanced at her bedside table clock and decided to let her answering machine screen the call. She had learned to be cautious about answering late at night.

After her recorded message and the sound of a beep, an apologetic voice began to speak. "Joanna, this is Pete. Sorry to call so late, but—"

She picked up the receiver. "Pete, I'm here."

"Joanna, uh, did I wake you?"

"Oh, no. I've just finished grading papers. I usually don't answer the phone in the late evenings, a precaution women living alone take sometimes."

"I see. I guess I'm not used to big city habits. Sounds like a good idea, though." He paused, cleared his throat. "How have you been?"

"Fine. And you?"

"Busy. It's that time of year on the farm."

"Oh?"

"Betsy told me what a great time she had visiting you."

"We both enjoyed it. I hope she'll come again soon."

"And she says you're coming to Greenville this weekend." He made it sound like a question, so she verified it.

"Yes, I'll be driving over Friday evening."

"That's what I'm calling about. I'd like you—and Betsy, too, of course—to come over on the Fourth for our annual cookout. My kids will be here, and we'll have fireworks and all the hoopla that goes with the occasion."

"Have you spoken to Betsy about it?" Joanna asked.

"Called her tonight, and she said it was okay with her if we agreed. How about it, Joanna, will you come?"

"It sounds like fun," Joanna said quickly. "Sure, count me in."

"Oh, and Joanna?"

"Yes?"

"Be sure to bring a bathing suit. We always spend some time in the pool."

"All right, Pete, I will."

"I'm sorry I waited so late to ask, Joanna. But I've been busy and..." He left the sentence unfinished. "Anyway, I'll see you this weekend. Drive carefully coming over."

"Good night, Pete." Joanna held the phone until the dial tone turned to a louder signal to alert the user to hang up the phone. A picnic at Pete's house. With all of his children. Maybe that would put Pete and her relationship to him in proper perspective, seeing him as the father of his large family. A pain so sharp it almost took away her breath caused Joanna to huddle miserably under the soft afghan, willing herself to shut out the images that crossed her mind. Why did she ever think seeing Pete again could put the ghosts of the past to rest? It had merely unchained them and now she was at their mercy. Sleep was slow to come even when she forced herself to turn out the light and deal with her demons in darkness.

****

"I wish I'd known earlier this was a potluck picnic. I'm embarrassed to arrive empty-handed," Joanna said as she backed her car out of Betsy's driveway.

"No need to be," Betsy assured her. "There'll be mountains of food left over, always is. Besides, you're our guest, so you aren't supposed to bring food."

"Do you think all of Pete's children will be there today?"

"I suppose so, except for Michael."

"It seems so strange that Pete has grownup children, and even grandchildren." Joanna drove slowly, almost reluctantly toward the neighboring farm. "And I have to confess, I'm a little nervous about meeting them. What if they don't like the idea of Pete going out with me and—"

"What's not to like? Their mother has been dead over three years so it's time their father got on with his life. They're good kids and I'm sure you'll get along great with all of them." When Joanna remained silent, she went on. "And with so many there, it will be like a zoo anyway. After the introductions, they'll probably forget you're not one of the family."

The black asphalt shimmered in the early afternoon sun and she remembered another Sunday not so long ago when she lay entangled in a bike on this road and Pete's warm hands caressed her injured ankle.

"Turn right here." Betsy's words brought Joanna abruptly back to the present and she made a sharp turn into the circular drive. As she shut off the ignition Pete came toward them in an open-necked cambric shirt and faded jeans, grinning broadly, and opened Betsy's door.

"Here you two are. Can I give you a hand with anything?"

"Just what we need." Betsy got out of the car, gave Pete a hug and motioned toward the trunk. "It's all back there."

He walked to the other side of the car.

"Hello, Joanna. How are you?" He touched her arm lightly but did not embrace her.

"Fine." Her warm brown eyes held his piercing blue gaze for a long moment.

"I'm glad you could come." His glance swept her white linen sun dress appreciatively.

"So am I." She smiled sincerely. "Thanks for inviting me."

"Good Lord, Bets, you didn't need to bring so much. The crowd's smaller than usual this year."

"Well, leftovers will keep. Maybe you won't have to cook for awhile." She gave a heavy casserole to Pete. "Watch out, that one's still warm."

Carrying the food, they made their way around the side of the house to the back door. "Girls," Pete called, "someone get the door for us."

"You called, Dad?" A pretty brunette appeared on the other side of the screen. "Oh, hi, Betsy." She smiled affectionately at her, then shot a quick curious glance at Joanna who was studying her with fascination. She opened the door and stood back to allow them to enter the kitchen. "Here, let me take some of that." She took a dish from Betsy, set it on the counter.

"Rebecca, this is Joanna." He smiled at each of them in turn. "And this is my older daughter,

Rebecca Elfrank."

"Hi." She extended her hand, realized Joanna still held a covered cake container, and reached for it. "I'll take that for you." She turned away as another brunette very much like her came across the room.

"And this is my younger daughter, LaWanda Acree."

Joanna turned her attention to the pregnant young woman who stood before her. "Hello."

LaWanda acknowledged the introduction with a quick smile.

"Don't ignore us, Dad." Two other women who had been busy at the stove came forward, smiling at Joanna. "We're the in-laws."

"I'm Ursula, the farmer's wife," said the one wearing a blond braid. "Kyle and I live just down the road. And this is the vet's wife. Ivana and Richard live in Sikeston. They're city people, too."

"Well, everything is relative," Ivana drawled, "so I guess compared to Greenville, we do live in a city."

"Ummm, look." Rebecca lifted the lid from the cake container. "Betsy's made her German Chocolate Cake. Our mother always said it wouldn't be the Fourth without it."

Pete cleared his throat. "Come on out to the patio, why don't you?" He looked at Joanna. "There's a crowd out there you need to meet, including a tribe of wild little Indians I call my grandkids."

"Are you coming, Betsy?" Joanna asked.

"In a little while, but you go on. I need to put some of the food in the fridge."

Joanna followed Pete through sliding glass doors. As he made the introductions, a small child ran up and grabbed him about his knees.

"Up, Gwampie," the child said and Pete stopped talking and lifted the little girl in his arms. "And this is Robin who belongs to LaWanda and Bill."

Joanna recognized the unmistakable features of a Down Syndrome child. "Hi, Robin." She touched the chubby hand that clung tightly to Pete's shoulder.

The child's head slowly swiveled and two almond-shaped eyes regarded her solemnly. "Gwammie?"

"No, honey, this is Joanna. She's Grampie's old, old friend."

"Well, not quite that old," Joanna said wryly and the others laughed.

"Right," Betsy's daughter-in-law chimed in. "I should look so good when I'm your age. Actually, I should look so good now."

"Thank you." Robin's sticky hand had taken hold of Joanna's and the child was still looking at her with avid attention.

"It's hard to believe you were in the class with this guy." Richard nodded toward Pete. "I guess having a family ages a person."

"You can say that again," Pete agreed, grinning at Joanna. He hugged Robin tighter and planted a kiss on top of her head. "But they're worth it."

"I'm sure they are," Joanna said wistfully as Robin twisted in Pete's embrace and held out her arms in an appealing gesture for Joanna to take her.

"May I?" Joanna looked at Pete.

"She's heavy," he warned.

"I can manage." Joanna took the child, settled her on one hip so that their faces were only inches apart.

"Kiss?" Robin puckered her mouth, closed her eyes.

Joanna laughed softly and kissed her moist cheek. "There." She pushed back a lock of Robin's dark hair and the little girl nestled contentedly against her.

"I think you just made a friend," Pete said

huskily and turned away before she could observe how it touched him to see Joanna with a child in her arms. By the time Pete introduced Joanna to everyone, the food had been ferried from the kitchen to the long folding tables set up in the tree-shaded back yard. Amid confusion and laughter everyone was finally seated and served. Betsy's cake and home-made ice cream completed the meal.

"What a feast. You ladies really outdid yourselves this time." Kyle placed an arm affectionately around his wife.

"Best picnic we've ever had," Pete agreed as he stood and began collecting the empty paper plates.

"Oh, Dad, you say that every year." LaWanda swiped at Robin's chocolate-smeared face with a damp napkin.

"And mean it sincerely. The larger our family grows, the more fun and fellowship."

"I agree," Betsy added, "though I'm afraid the DeBolt family has shrunk a bit this year."

"Yes, last year Walt was still with us," Rebecca sighed, "and not so long ago, our mother, too."

"I just meant—" Betsy began but was interrupted by Pete.

"Say, why don't we go for a dip in the pool and cool off while the young ones are taking a break to settle their lunches?" He looked at Joanna and Betsy, then Kyle. "Anyone game?"

"Not me." Kyle shook his head. "I've been drafted to help Ursula referee the video cartoon crowd. And Richard and Bill are taking on Spencer and Lee pitching horseshoes."

"They'll need the referee," Ivana predicted wryly, then turned to Pete. "Sorry, Dad, but I'm helping get the little ones down for naps." She joined Betsy's daughter-in-law who was already rounding up small children amid various sounds of protest.

"You-all go ahead, Dad," Rebecca said. "I'm

going to put the food away and get the kitchen cleaned up, then I'll join you."

"We'll help," Joanna and Betsy said in unison.

"I'll help, too," LaWanda told her, "soon as I get this one bedded down. Come on, Robin, let's go."

"No, me fim." Robin looked to Pete for support.

"Not right now, sweetheart." He swept her up in his arms. "Let's go inside and Grampie will read you a story before you take your nap." He looked at Joanna. "See you at the pool in a little while."

"He's good with children," Betsy said softly as they watched Pete walk toward the house, LaWanda following. "And that one is special to him."

"How old is she?" Joanna asked.

"Almost five. But children like her are several years behind in their development."

In the kitchen, Betsy tied on an apron and began filling the sink with water as she handed Joanna a dish towel. "I'll wash, you dry."

"Dad said you teach English at Memphis State," Rebecca said as she scraped pans and gave them to Betsy. "I guess small town life seems pretty dull by comparison."

"Not at all," Joanna said truthfully. "I've always loved Greenville."

"But I'm sure you'd be bored to tears living here after big city life," Rebecca persisted.

"Oh, no, I—" She stopped, aware that she was being backed into a corner. She smiled warmly at Pete's elder daughter. "Life is what you make it, Rebecca. It doesn't matter where you are, it's who you are that counts."

Rebecca had the grace to blush and turn her full attention to her task.

Betsy dried her hands. "Well, let's put on our swim suits."

"I left mine in the car," Joanna told her. "I'll get it and join you in the house."

CHAPTER SIX

Joanna walked slowly across the yard, savoring the sounds of children's laughter mixed with the noise of the videotape that came from the covered patio, the ring of horseshoes hitting iron stakes as shouts and groans from the young men accompanied their game. Family fun and fellowship, Pete had said. All of these years, this had been his while she had ached for just one child. She tried to imagine Mary Esther as part of the picture. How lucky she had been.

Retrieving her beach bag, Joanna let herself in the front door and walked toward the kitchen.

"Why did she suddenly show up now?" Joanna's steps slowed at the sound of Rebecca's voice.

"Maybe she heard about our mother and thought the time was right to make a move on Dad," LaWanda suggested. "Betsy said they dated all through high school, until she moved away."

"I thought, after Walt died, your dad and Betsy..." Ivana left the sentence unfinished and Rebecca spoke again.

"Don't we wish. Betsy's already like a member of the family. And we know our mother would have wanted that."

"They do seem more compatible," Ivana observed. "The farm, and church, their families growing up together."

"Right, and *she's* a single college professor." LaWanda agreed. "Wonder why she never married? She seems to like kids."

"Probably just an act, to impress Dad."

"Have you girls seen Joanna?" Betsy's voice joined the others. "I thought she was coming in to change."

"No, Betsy," LaWanda answered. "Say, don't you look nice. Is that a new suit?"

"Sure is. Got it in Cape this weekend when Joanna and I went to the mall."

Joanna entered the kitchen with a determined smile. "Where do I go to change into my swim suit?"

The four women turned toward the sound of her voice. "Down the hall, first door on the right," Betsy told her. "Meet you at the pool."

She walked through the hallway toward the door. Betsy had directed her to the master suite. On the walnut triple dresser, two large framed photographs faced, one of Pete, the other Mary Esther. She tip-toed closer, studied the woman's face. The picture had obviously been made several years ago, judging by its companion pose of Pete, but she had been as pretty as Joanna remembered the teen-aged girl to be. Pete's wife, the woman who had borne his children, made a home for him. She thought of the conversation she'd overheard just now. It would take time to win over Pete's daughters. But she had patience and plenty of experience dealing with difficult young people. Only this time it was not easy to be objective.

Joanna changed into her suit and joined Pete and Betsy at the pool, and felt his keen blue eyes rove her body with frank approval.

"You look great, Joanna. Betsy was just telling me that you two bought new suits on your shopping trip yesterday." Joanna nodded and he went on. "I wanted to stop by this weekend after you came, but

I've been tied up with school business."

"Betsy told me about that yesterday." Joanna eased into the pool, feeling relief as the cool water covered her from Pete's gaze that was like a caress. "Sounds like you have a difficult job on your hands."

"Nothing I can't handle but it's taking a lot of my time." Pete dove under, came up spraying water. "But this is a holiday. Let's forget that for now. Come on, last one to the other end of the pool gets ducked."

Joanna pushed off from the side of the pool and caught up with her two old friends as they swam into deeper water, laughing and splashing. She was determined to make the best of the day.

Throughout the remainder of the afternoon the two families engaged in their familiar holiday rituals which included eating watermelons accompanied by a seed spitting contest which Pete handily won. Joanna laughed until tears ran down her cheeks as she and Bets paired off in a three-legged race against the younger women.

"You've got the longest legs," Betsy complained as they hopped to the finish line last, "so we should've won."

"I can't help it if your short legs held us back," Joanna retorted with a giggle.

"Girls, girls." Pete put an arm around each of them. "No bickering. It's not whether you win or lose—" They joined him to finish, "it's how you play the game."

Snacks were served and dishes collected by their various owners. The last of the sleepy children had been hugged and tucked into cars and minivans for the trips home, and the grownups were saying their goodbyes.

"Fantastic fireworks, guys."

"We'll get together again soon."

"Nice to meet you, Joanna."

"Learn how to pitch horseshoes before the next holiday, will you, Lee?"

"It'll be too cold for horseshoes on Thanksgiving. I'll work on my dart game."

"Great picnic, Dad. Come for supper one night this week."

"If I can." Pete turned to look at Betsy and Joanna as cars began to drive away. "It's early yet. Why don't you two stay for awhile?"

"I think I'd like to get on home, Pete. But Joanna doesn't have to go." As Joanna opened her mouth to protest, Betsy went on. "I'll just take your car, and Pete can drop you off whenever you want to come back." She laughed. "I won't set a curfew. And I promise I won't wait up. All that swimming and running races has worn me out." She held out her hand and Joanna dug into her bag for car keys and gave them to her.

"Would you like to sit out by the pool?" Pete asked and when she nodded, led the way to a cushioned glider on the flagstone patio. Sitting down, he continued, "Well, what did you think of them?"

"You have a wonderful family, Pete," Joanna said sincerely. "I'm not sure I've figured out who belongs to who but they're all children to be proud of, yours and Betsy's, too." She was acutely aware of Pete's arm resting on the back of the glider almost touching her shoulder.

"I've missed seeing you the last few weeks, Joanna." Pete's voice was apologetic. "But this is a busy time on the farm and then there were all the school problems."

"I've been busy, too."

A full moon had risen and the night sounds and scents made Joanna suddenly feel transported back to Greenville in an earlier time of her life.

"Reminds me of your front porch at the

parsonage," Pete said softly.

So he feels it, too, Joanna thought. After all those years with Mary Esther and his family, he still holds to the same memories I do.

Pete reached for her hand, whispered huskily, "And reminds me of that kid who was so enamored with the minister's daughter."

"And she was star struck by the hero of the basketball court."

He pulled her gently into his arms, cupped her moon-drenched face in his hands, and looked at her a long moment before he bent to kiss her. His mouth moved over hers in a tentative way until sensing her response, he parted her lips and probed deeply inside with his tongue. One hand on the small of her back, his other began to explore the enticing curves of her breasts. She stroked the back of his neck, the side of his jaw, her breath coming in short gasps as the fire between them flared, suffusing her whole body.

"Let's go inside," Pete mumbled thickly against her ear.

Before she could respond to his words, a car pulled into the circular driveway, its headlights making a wide arc above the high fence.

Pete swore softly. "Somebody probably forgot something. I'll take care of it." He opened the gate and she could hear his footsteps on the flagstone walk as he went toward the front.

"Hey, Pete. Where is everybody?"

"Already gone home. You're a little late for the picnic, Boyd."

"Just as well. What I came to say needs to be kept between the two of us."

Behind the fence where their voices could be heard clearly, Joanna made a motion to stand, then checked herself. Any noise might alert Boyd to her presence and she wasn't sure whether Pete would want him to know she was here. Whatever he had to say was safe with her. After all, she had no stake in Greenville's problems now.

"Thel and I went to the town center picnic today and we've been kicking this around and decided you ought to know what's happening."

"Well?"

"People around here are getting ugly about the elementary school issue. Formed a committee today to try and stop the merger. Even started a smear campaign against you. And they're looking for anything they can use so watch your step."

"Good God, who's behind all this?"

"I don't want to say, Pete. But it's a low-down way of fighting—going behind a guy's back when he's done as much for this community as you have."

"Well, thanks, Boyd, but I don't guess there's much I can do about this except ignore the flak. Most things work out for the best in the end."

"I hope you're right. Guess I'd better get home now."

"Thanks for passing this on, Boyd. Say hello to Thel for me."

Pete came back and sank wearily onto the glider."You heard?"

"Yes, but the conversation is safe with me."

"I know that. And I half expected this would happen." He sighed. "I've angered the Catholic community on this issue but the town can't continue to support separate schools. Any fool can see that."

"Some people will fight change even in their best interest."

"If it's a fight they want, then so be it." He made a fist, socked the palm of his hand with it. "It *will* be done."

"Not if they vote it down at the polls, Pete," Joanna said softly.

He took her hand and grinned at her. "I'm

grateful for Boyd's information but his timing was lousy. Now where were we before he interrupted?"

Joanna thought of Boyd's words. A smear campaign against Pete. Would their relationship be something to be used against him? For his sake, she couldn't afford to take that chance.

Pete reached for her again but she didn't respond.

"We mustn't do this, Pete," she said gently.

"Why?" He sounded puzzled.

"Because...I should go, Pete. I have to leave very early in the morning and drive back to Memphis."

He stood and faced her. "I'm sorry I misread you, Joanna. I thought you were feeling what I was." When she remained silent, he added brusquely, "I'll get the keys and meet you at the car."

After Pete left her, Joanna stood for a moment staring at the moon's reflection in the dark water of the pool. She could still feel his hands pressing her body against him, his breath warm in her ear as he whispered words of love. If only she could have responded with all of her aching need to show the overwhelming love she felt for him. But Boyd Bernard's words had shattered the moment of fulfillment and she knew they must be cautious. Pete had too much to lose if their indiscretion became known but there was no way she could explain that to him tonight.

CHAPTER SEVEN

A knock at the front door startled Pete as he sat dozing with a newspaper in his lap. He glanced at his watch, frowned, and went to answer it.

"Bets, hello." He opened the door wider, stepped back. "Come on in. What brings you out so late?"

"I've been babysitting Spencer's lively bunch tonight so I stopped by to let you know what I overheard in the drugstore today."

"Come sit down and tell me about it. Coffee?"

"No, thanks." Betsy shook her head, remained standing.

"Of course, I know there's not a bit of truth in it but just the same, you ought to be aware..." Betsy stopped, seeming reluctant to repeat the words that she had come to say, then went on. "Two women from church were discussing the school merger. One said she had it on good authority that you had money invested in the construction company that the Board awarded the contract to build the new high school."

"Hell fire, Betsy! The bids were sealed and I only had one vote, just like all the rest."

"I know it doesn't make any sense, Pete, and that's what I butted in and told her but some people believe anything they hear and this kind of story could hurt the vote on consolidation in November."

"Hurt it?" He spat out the words in disgust. "It

will kill it."

"It makes me mad as the devil for anyone to accuse you of wrongdoing."

"I appreciate your vote of confidence, Bets. It's hard for me to believe anyone in this community would be spreading lies like that. If I could get my hands on the..." He clenched his fists, shrugged helplessly and let them fall back to his sides.

"I'll be going." Betsy yawned. "I have to freeze apples tomorrow."

Pete grinned. "Thanks for telling me, old friend."

As Pete closed the door, the phone rang and he went to the kitchen to answer, his face relaxing into a wide grin when he recognized the familiar voice.

"I hope I'm not calling too late?" Joanna asked.

"No, in fact, if you'd called a minute earlier you could have said hello to Betsy. She just left."

"Oh?"

The word sounded like a question but Pete didn't explain before he asked, "How are you?"

"Fine. I was just wondering if you'd like to drive over this weekend and have dinner. That is, if you aren't too busy?"

"Great. Saturday night? Would you like to make the reservations? Same place as before, or wherever you prefer?"

"I thought we'd just stay here and I'd make dinner."

"Well, sure, if you like but you don't have to cook for me, Joanna. I know you spend a lot of time at the college."

"It won't be any trouble, Pete. Just something simple," she assured him.

After some talk about their respective activities, they agreed on a time for Saturday and Pete hung up the phone. He'd thought a lot about what happened by the pool last weekend and he still couldn't figure it out. Joanna had been so loving and then all of a sudden, nothing. Almost like he'd felt at her place.

Wait a minute, he said slowly to himself. Maybe that was it. She'd been full of passion until he suggested going inside. Did the idea of making love in the house he'd shared with Mary Esther repel her? In the same bed perhaps? Or had she gotten carried away by the moonlit moment and then suddenly remembered who they both were and rejected him? If the weekend in Memphis turned out the way he hoped, he'd have his answer.

To Pete the days seemed more like weeks until Saturday finally came and he was standing in the hallway at Beekman Place waiting for Joanna to answer her doorbell. He was wearing new slacks and a navy striped shirt and feeling more comfortable in his casual attire than if he was dressed for dinner out.

Joanna answered the bell on first ring and stood in the open door with the sun shining through the long windows behind her, making a halo around her dark hair.

"Hello, Pete." She smiled warmly. "Come in."

He bent to brush her lips lightly as their eyes met, held for a long moment, then he gave her the bouquet of yellow roses. "I thought you might like these."

"Oh, Pete, they're beautiful." She buried her face in their heady fragrance.

"Not as beautiful as you," he answered softly and followed her into the living room.

She smoothed her jade linen pants with a slight nod of acknowledgement. "Let me get a vase and put them on the table."

She went to the kitchen to fill the crystal container with water. "Would you like some wine before dinner?"

"Yes, thank you." He followed her. "May I help?"

She motioned to the bottle chilling in an ice bucket. "I'd consider it a big favor if you'd pop the cork. I've been known to spray the ceiling."

Pete poured the Zinfandel and stood watching as she arranged the flowers. God, she was a desirable woman. He'd like to skip the wine and dinner and take her straight to bed, but he'd play it by the rules. There was no rush. They had all night ahead of them.

Joanna lit the candles, and put on a cassette, then served the salad.

"Umm. Quite a tangy flavor."

"Do you like it?" Joanna looked anxious.

"Very much," he assured her with all the sincerity he could muster through puckered lips.

When they finished, she brought servings of beef stroganoff and fresh broccoli casserole.

He took a mouthful, chewed, swallowed. "Interesting."

"It's sprinkled with alfalfa, for extra fiber."

Alfalfa? Cattle feed? He made a point of taking a second bite before he pronounced it delicious. He took a muffin from the basket Joanna offered, and buttered a piece of it.

"Wonderful muffins. Did you bake them?"

"They're homemade," Joanna answered, then added, "It's Eve's recipe. They're flavored with licorice root and hawthorn berries, to lower cholesterol."

"Great." Pete nodded approvingly. Eve's recipes. That explained everything.

For dessert, they had espresso and banana-orange cake, made with oat bran, Joanna told him and pointed out its nutritional advantages. *Oat bran? Horse feed?* Feeling that if he had to indulge in one more healthy mouthful he would surely choke, Pete complimented Joanna on her culinary efforts and offered to help clear the dishes.

"Well, if you really want to," Joanna said.

They worked companionably in her kitchen, Pete scraping and rinsing, Joanna loading the dishwasher, then returned to the living room. The candles still burned on the table, giving the room its only light and the low music from the stereo completed the romantic mood.

"Let's dance, Joanna." Pete held out his hand and she came to him and melted into his arms. They moved with the music, eyes closed, aware of the growing tension between them, with the unspoken knowledge that this was the night when they would fulfill their fantasies. Pete's hand caressed Joanna's back, sliding sensuously over the silk fabric of her blouse. "You feel so wonderful. I love to touch you," he whispered in her ear. They gave up any pretense of dancing and stood for a long moment just holding each other, lost in time. Then slowly he lifted her face, memorized her shining dark hair that framed it, her silver earrings catching the candle glow, her eyes that sparkled with their own warm lights. He bent to softly kiss her lips but when their mouths touched, it was as though the flame from the candle caught fire and they were burning together, their passion blazing out of control.

"Joanna," Pete whispered urgently, molding her against him so that he could feel the curves of her soft voluptuous body against the muscular hardness of his own.

"Pete, let's—" Her words were drowned out by the ringing of the phone.

For a moment they stood still, shocked by the shrill intrusion into their private world. Then she reluctantly pulled away and went to answer it.

Pete took a few steps and sat down on the sofa, cursing Alexander Graham Bell in absentia; then something in the tone of Joanna's voice told him the call was not a social one. Surely not one of his children...? He got up and went to stand beside her.

"Yes, I understand. Yes, I'll be there as soon as possible." She looked at Pete and shook her head to let him know there was no need for him to be concerned. "Yes, please do call the doctor now."

Putting the phone in its cradle, she explained quickly. "That was the convalescent home where my mother lives. She's fallen and they aren't sure how badly she's hurt. I need to go over there right away."

"I'll take you," Pete said.

"Let me get my handbag, I'll just be a minute."

Pete blew out the candles and turned off the stereo while he waited for Joanna to return, casting one final look at the romantic setting which he knew was her way of saying yes to everything he had hoped the evening would bring.

Joanna gave directions to Oakwood Manor. They were silent as Pete concentrated on getting there as quickly as possible.

"My mother has been here about four years now," Joanna explained as they reached the entrance to the sprawling red brick building. "She doesn't remember much so don't be surprised that she doesn't recognize you. Most of the time she doesn't even know me."

"It's all right," Pete said gently. "I understand. I won't expect anything."

They stopped at the desk and the nurse on duty smiled at them. "You certainly made good time."

Joanna acknowledged the remark with a nod and asked, "How is she?"

"The doctor has seen her and thinks nothing is broken. But he's ordered x-rays just to be sure. She'll have to go to the hospital for that."

Joanna nodded again.

"She's pretty shaken up, and we've had a hard time keeping her in bed. I'm glad you're here, she's always calmer when you're around."

Joanna hurried down the hallway, Pete following close behind. At the last door, she paused, looked at Pete. "Let me go first and talk to her a bit."

Pete wouldn't have recognized the shriveled old woman who lay restrained to the narrow bed, whimpering pitifully.

"Mother, it's me, Joanna. I know you've had a fall but it's going to be okay. The doctor says you haven't any broken bones."

"I hurt." The voice was that of a petulant child, not the rich southern accent Pete remembered.

"I brought someone to see you." Joanna stroked her mother's arm and looked toward Pete, motioning him inside the room.

Mrs. Flemming's eyes followed the direction of Joanna's gaze, then she suddenly stiffened and began to scream.

"Mother, it's Pete. You remember Peter Damron? From Greenville?"

The woman's eyes on Pete were wild with fear and she thrashed back and forth in her restraints with enough strength to test their limits. "No!" She averted her eyes, screamed again, "No!" then began jabbering incomprehensibly to Joanna.

"Mother, it's all right." Joanna looked quickly at Pete and shook her head. He backed out of the door just as two nurses came running to investigate the disturbance.

When the woman was calmer, Joanna joined him in the hall. "I'm sorry, Pete, I shouldn't have asked you to come in. She is sometimes afraid of strangers."

She knew me, Pete thought with conviction. And she certainly wasn't glad to see me again.

"It's okay, Joanna." Pete touched her arm gently.

"I'll have to go along to the hospital." She looked regretful. "It may take several hours."

"I understand. I'll go with you and wait to take you home."

"You don't need to do that. I can call Eve or take a cab."

"The wait won't seem so long if you're not alone. You might need me and I want to be there for you, Joanna."

"If you're sure?"

He lightly touched her cheek. "I'm sure."

They followed the ambulance to Methodist Hospital where Joanna completed admission forms; then stayed with her mother in an emergency cubicle until she was taken for x-rays.

Pete sat alone in the deserted waiting room, idly thumbing through a tattered copy of Newsweek. But his mind was not on the pages in front of him. He kept thinking of the frail elderly woman who became hysterical at the sight of him a while ago. He had always felt that Mrs. Flemming liked him and approved of him dating her daughter so why the sudden outburst? She had acted as though she thought he meant to harm her. He supposed it didn't mean anything since Joanna said the poor woman's mind was gone but just the same, it was spooky.

"Pete?"

Joanna was standing in front of him. "I'm sorry this is taking so long. They said it might be a few hours before we know the results of the x-rays."

"No problem." He moved to one side of the sofa and motioned her to sit down. "Would you like a cup of coffee or a cola?"

"Coffee would be nice, thank you." She settled into the space beside him. "This isn't how I'd planned to entertain you this evening." She gestured at their surroundings with a wry smile.

He grinned back at her. "We're together, aren't we? That's enough for me."

"You always said that when we sat in the porch

swing under the disapproving eyes of my father, didn't you?"

"And meant it sincerely." He stood. "I'll get that coffee now."

He returned with two paper cups and a couple of candy bars. "We need to keep up our energy level, too," he explained.

"I need no excuse for chocolate." Joanna tore into the wrapper and took a large bite, leaving a dark trace of it on her lower lip.

Just as he was fighting his impulse to lick it off, a nurse approached them.

"Flemming?"

"Yes?" Joanna stood quickly, almost overturning her drink.

"Your mama is back from x-ray now, but she's sedated and sleeping. You can just wait here with your husband and we'll call you when we know anything."

"He's not—thank you," Joanna finished lamely and sat down.

I could have been her husband now if only...he left the words unfinished. There was no need to beat a dead horse. The past was done.

"I suppose being here brings back painful memories for you, Pete. I shouldn't have allowed you to come."

She would be surprised to know that his painful memories at the moment were of her, he thought, as he answered. "Well, hospitals are not on my list of favorite places but I've spent my share of time in them."

After a moment, she said softly, "Will you tell me about it, Pete?"

He had not spoken of his feelings about Mary Esther's death to anyone until now. He had shared his children's grief with them, offering what solace he could. He had commiserated with friends, reminding them of all the happy times they'd spent together. But his own loss had remained his private sorrow and it was hard to put it into words.

Finally, he said, "I miss her. She was part of my life for a long time and I loved her."

He looked at Joanna."You remembered Mary Esther's long hair? She was proud of that, called it her best feature. But the radiation made it fall out in huge clumps. And they kept hitting her with treatments trying to stop the damned cancer that was eating her up. She couldn't bear to look at her bald head and she didn't want anyone else to see her that way."

He shook his head in frustration and took a deep breath.

"She was a good person and I hated to see her suffering and humiliation." He made a fist and hit the palm of his hand—hard. "But there wasn't a damned thing I could do about it. That's what hurt the most. I was totally helpless to stop what was happening. I failed her."

He put his head in his hands and felt his tears come—slowly at first, then in a great rush as his shoulders heaved with silent sobs.

Joanna knelt in front of him and wrapped her arms around him. She rocked him in a gentle motion that soothed his tense body and soon he was quiet. "Pete, Pete. You didn't fail her. I'm sure you were there for her as much as any husband could have been."

He swiped at his eyes and raised his head. "You didn't need this. I'm sorry."

"Don't be," she whispered. "I asked you to tell me and I'm glad you did."

"Can you understand when I say I loved my wife, but not in the way I loved you?"

"I think so."

"And I had a happy life with her and with our

children but that I never forgot you or what we had together?"

Joanna nodded.

"But that phase of my life is over now. I'm ready to move on. Life is for the living and I feel very much alive now that I've found you again." He sat up and pulled her onto the seat beside him and put his arms around her.

They sat entwined, cheek to cheek, not speaking until they dozed. And that was how the nurse found them two hours later when she returned to tell them the report was good and they were free to go.

CHAPTER EIGHT

Pete opened the door to Bernard's Barber Shop and stepped in from the sweltering heat. The cool air and conversation hit him simultaneously.

"And as I told 'em over at the hardware store, we don't need any merger that keeps our kids from getting religious education. And if the damned School Board tries to force—" Boyd swiveled the heavyset man's chair to face the door and he stopped in mid-sentence. "Why, hello, Pete."

"Hank." He nodded to Boyd and turned toward the row of leather chairs where Al Mittendorf sat thumbing through an old copy of The Farm Journal. "Hey, Al. I didn't expect you to be here. Got your corn picked already?"

"Not quite. Vada's over at the Kut-N-Kurl getting all prettied up so I thought I'd just get a haircut and wait it out here in the shop."

Boyd motioned for Pete to take the vacated chair, fastened the plastic cape. "The usual?" he asked.

Pete hesitated. "I thought you might leave it a little longer at the neck. And maybe the sideburns, too?" He had considered going into Sikeston and having his hair styled but out of loyalty to his old friend, had decided against it.

"This merger issue is getting hotter," Al said with a sidelong glance at Pete. "What does the Board plan to do if it's voted down?"

"If that happens, we'll deal with it," Pete answered with a shrug.

"Hold still now," Boyd cautioned, "unless you want one of those wedge cuts like the kids are wearing."

"Seen Joanna lately?" Al asked.

"Couple of weeks ago."

"Well, hell, that doesn't sound like you're serious about the woman. You used to sit on her front porch every evening if I remember right."

"It's a little farther to Memphis than the parsonage," Pete answered. "Besides, she's teaching classes this summer."

"Vada was hoping she'd come for a visit soon. She wants to get the girls together for lunch at our house."

"I think she'd like that. I'll mention it to her when we talk."

Al stood. "Here comes my wife. Wonder what that fancy hairdo cost me today?"

"More than your trim, but she looks better than you do," Boyd said with a grin.

"That'll cost you a tip next time, buddy." Al paused at the door. "See you, guys."

Pete watched through the mirror as Al and Vada met on the sidewalk, linked arms, and walked toward the parking lot. He tried to imagine Joanna and himself in their place, but somehow couldn't visualize Joanna patronizing the Kut-N-Kurl.

"Going to Memphis this weekend?" Boyd asked when they were alone.

"I don't know yet. It depends."

Boyd snipped a few more uneven hairs, then handed him a mirror. "What do you think?"

He checked the back. "Looks good, thanks." He gave Boyd a couple dollars more than his regular tip after he removed the cape and whisked his neck.

"Thank you." As Pete reached the door, Boyd spoke again. "Pete? Remember what I said. Watch your step."

He nodded and went out into the stifling air. Feeling thirsty, he decided to stop by Shonoff's for a cold beer before he drove home.

As he passed Yokeley's Drugs he could almost hear the jukebox playing after school and see Joanna and her girlfriends sitting at the fountain sipping cokes. And when the guys came in they would all go to the back and dance until time to go home for dinner. And afterward he'd hang out at the parsonage until her father called her inside for devotionals before bed.

When he stepped inside Shonoff's a group of men were shooting pool and Hank, with his back to the door, was saying, "...so I told 'em at the barber shop that we didn't intend to let that merger go through if it took—"

Pete turned and quietly left the building. Suddenly, he wanted to get home and call Joanna more than he wanted a cold beer.

He let the phone ring until the answering machine began its prerecorded message and hung up. Joanna was probably still at the university so he wouldn't try her cell phone now. He had that cold beer, sitting on his patio and thinking of the night she stayed after the picnic. It had seemed to be the moment to fulfill all his fantasies until Boyd's untimely interruption. And then at her apartment, they'd resumed where they left off but her mother's accident had jinxed his hopes again. If he were a superstitious man, he'd think this relationship was never meant to be.

He finished his beer and went inside to watch a farm show that dealt with cotton prices. This was predicted to be a good year and he had planted extra fields to take advantage of that.

Later he tried Joanna's number again without success. It was after four and her classes ended at one so he tried her cell phone this time. She answered on the fourth ring.

"Hello, Joanna. Pete here."

"Hello."

"I tried your house phone but I guess you're not there yet. Is your mother still doing okay?"

"Yes, she's fine. Well, not fine but the same as before her fall."

Instead of her customary warm response to his call, Joanna's voice sounded flat. "Is everything all right?"

"Yes. Just the usual end of semester craziness."

"I was thinking, how about if I come over tomorrow night and take you to dinner? To celebrate the end of the week or something?"

"That sounds lovely, Pete, but I just can't spare the time right now. Grades have to be in by Wednesday and I'm nowhere near to finishing."

"All work and no play, you know."

She gave an audible sigh. "I know about work but play is not part of my life right now. I've got a list of students to help with fall scheduling and only three more days to do it."

"You do take time to eat, don't you?" he asked in a tone that was half jest, half concern.

She gave a short laugh. "I had lunch in the cafeteria but I'm not leaving my office for another few hours. I'll grab a sandwich on the way home. Meanwhile, I'll manage with coffee and maybe a Power Bar."

"Joanna, I don't think—" he began.

"Not to worry. This is routine. I've survived it before. Look, I'm sorry but I have to hang up now. I've got a student waiting to see her faculty advisor—that's me."

"Right, call me when you have a chance.

Goodbye."

He stood holding the phone, frustration causing him to grip the receiver until the dial tone reminded him to hang up.

Damn, the woman was driving herself to exhaustion. He'd recognized the tiredness in her voice and she was determined to continue in spite of it. He had the urge to go yank her out of that office and lavish some tender loving care on her. Well, why not? He glanced at his watch. In little more than two hours, he could do just that.

Pete roared out of his driveway as if the hounds of hell were after him. He could make good time until he reached the city limits of Memphis and then he'd have to adjust his speed to the flow of city traffic.

It didn't occur to him to question his impulsive action until he was almost to the university. What if Joanna wasn't glad to see him? What if she considered his impromptu appearance an unwelcome surprise? Then he'd just have to convince her otherwise. She needed him right now, whether she realized it or not. And he wouldn't let her down.

He parked near the center of the university complex and asked the first student he saw for directions to the English building. Red brick structures of various height and age were crowded together on the sprawling campus, the Patterson Building prominent among them.

Pete stopped for a moment before mounting the steps to the entrance. So this was Joanna's world, the place where she worked at the job level she had spent years attaining and obviously loved.

He squared his shoulders and went inside. A directory in the hallway told him the faculty offices were located on the second floor. A couple of students passed him on their way down the stairs as he went up. At the door he hesitated, then seeing a muscular young man sitting in a row of chairs along one wall, he went in and sat down, too.

The student looked up, then twisted nervously in his chair.

"You here for Dr. Flemming, too?" he asked.

Pete nodded.

"Yeah, dumb question. Everybody else left an hour ago. Even if they didn't get to all their appointments. But Doc Flemming is staying to see every one of hers."

Pete nodded again. He didn't suppose the student considered it odd that he was not a kid since many older teachers went back to summer school each year.

"She's been my advisor since I transferred from Waycross to play football. Helped me get all my credits counted. Toward my major." He ran a hand through his close-cropped sandy hair. "But this time, I may be asking for more than even Dr. Flemming can handle."

Pete cocked an eyebrow and waited.

"See, I've got to keep a B average for football and I just flunked World History. That's got me under the gun with Coach and if the doc can't help me, I'm off the team."

Before Pete could answer, Joanna's door opened and a girl came out carrying an armful of books. She gestured toward the office. "Next."

The student rose and disappeared inside. Pete sat staring at the closed door, wondering how long this appointment would take. In the quiet room, he could hear the voices from within.

"So I've got to bring up my GPA before fall semester or I lose the scholarship. And I was hoping, Doctor Flemming, maybe you'd be willing to change my C in English Lit to an A and I'd make it?"

"I'm sorry, Ted. I can't do that." After a long silence, she went on. "The university offers two weeks of interim classes before regular term. I'm teaching a course on Short Stories. You could ace that."

"Day classes?"

"Yes, they meet from nine to three."

"But I've got a job and I'll need the money to pay expenses my scholarship won't cover."

Another long silence followed, then he heard Joanna say, "Okay, Ted, here's what I can offer. You sign up for the course, read all the material, complete the assignments. And meet me at Student Union a couple of evenings a week for review. Can you manage that?"

"You better believe it. And thanks, Doctor Flemming, thanks a lot."

"You're welcome. I wouldn't want to deprive the team of its most promising player."

There was the sound of a chair scraping on the floor and footsteps. The door opened and Ted turned back—"See you at registration—" then flashed a wide grin and thumbs up sign at Pete as he lumbered past.

Pete walked toward Joanna's office and hesitated. She sat hunched over her desk, head in hands, surrounded by stacks of papers. He knocked softly and she turned, startled, but at the sight of him, her face lit up.

"Pete, what on earth—"

He walked toward her, planted a quick kiss on her forehead, put his hands on her shoulders and began slowly massaging her taut muscles. "You work too hard, my love. I've come to take you away from all this for a brief reprieve."

"But I've already explained—"

"Shhhh." He put a finger to her lips, then turned her chair to face her desk and resumed his task. "If you're going to be a workhorse, someone has to take care of you. Even the best of them have to be fed and watered and exercised daily and that is precisely what I've come to do."

Joanna laughed.

Pete looked down and marveled that he had forgotten that low musical quality in her laughter. Her mouth opened and she tilted her head back.

"What?" he asked.

"If you're comparing me to a horse, I think you should check my teeth to be sure I'm sound and not some old gray mare."

Pete chuckled, lowered his head and kissed her right on her open mouth. "You're more than sound and you aren't an old gray mare. Trust me." He deepened the kiss for a few sensual seconds before she backed away with a sigh.

"These grades have to—" She gestured helplessly toward the pile of test papers in front of her, then closed her eyes and sighed, "ooooh, that feels wonderful."

"So just relax for a moment." His thumbs gently circled the plains of her shoulders, then traced the contour of her spine from neck to waist and back. He brushed aside the collar of her blouse and softly kissed the nape of her graceful neck.

"Mmmmmmm. If I relax any more than this, I'll fall asleep."

"I'd bet the farm you haven't slept much lately. What am I to do with you, Joanna?"

"Whatever you wish. After this massage, I'm at your service."

Pete chuckled. "Okay, first we'll get a bite to eat, somewhere close by. And then we'll walk a bit. I've never seen the campus before, you know."

"All right, Pete, I'll come with you. It's the least I can do after you've driven all the way from Greenville."

"I owed you one, Joanna, after that night at the hospital. This is my way of saying thanks."

She stood and he embraced her, then remembered where they were and reluctantly released her.

"There's a coffee shop at the Student Union Building across campus. They serve good sandwiches. And I can show you part of the university on the way."

"Sounds good to me. I'm getting hungry, too. I haven't had anything since a beer this afternoon."

They strolled across the well-manicured grounds with Joanna calling attention to the different buildings.

"On the right is Overton Hall, that's where Eve teaches. We share the same parking lot."

Pete nodded and took her hand. "I'm glad I came today. Now when I think of you at work, I'll be able to picture you here."

"Just as I can visualize you on the farm."

"Yeah."

"And over there is the new athletic complex with the football field farther on."

"That student who just left your office; he said he played football on a scholarship."

"Ted? Yes, but he's in danger of losing it because of his grades."

"I had a basketball scholarship from SEMO."

"Yes, I remember."

"We talked about going there together, remember? But money was scarce and there weren't many grants or loans available then and the scholarship didn't cover nearly all the cost. Going into the army offered a chance to enroll later on the GI Bill." He shrugged. "But when I came back it didn't seem important anymore. Until now."

"You would have been a great asset to SEMO or any college, Pete, with your athletic ability."

"It's not the glory of the basketball court I regret missing, Joanna. I just wish I had the education, the degree, the ring to show for it. But I guess it wouldn't benefit a Missouri cotton farmer all that much, would it?"

"You have everything you need, Pete. A successful farm, a wonderful family, a leadership role in the community."

"Enough about me and my hang-ups." He grinned at her. "I came to distract you from this course toward collapse you seem hell-bent on following."

Joanna laughed. "I do this at the end of every semester. Tests to be graded. Kids desperate for points they haven't earned. Impossible schedules to arrange for next semester. And the pressure to get it all done yesterday."

"So why do it?" Pete asked with a puzzled frown.

"Because I love my work." Her face grew animated as she spoke. "It's rewarding to make a difference in young people's lives."

Pete nodded. "The world needs more teachers like you, Doctor Flemming."

The shadows of the tall oaks lengthened as they walked on in companionable silence. There were few students about at this hour and he considered taking her hand but checked himself for fear of compromising her image should they be observed.

A tall, dark-haired girl came toward them as they approached the Student Union. She wore jeans and a halter top and even in the dusk, her full lips caught his attention. It could have been a young Joanna, so familiar she looked.

He turned toward her as they neared the door. "I guess you will think this foolish, but I'm going to tell you anyway. All these years, I stared at girls like that one who remind me of you and thought, 'That could be Joanna's daughter.' And I've had a strong urge to stop them and ask if they belong to you."

Her quick intake of breath startled him. She

turned her face away and walked up the steps so quickly he had to rush to catch up and open the door for her. Did he say something wrong? Maybe she felt his words were a putdown of her single status. Maybe he'd hit a raw nerve at her never having children of her own. Whatever brought on the reaction he wished to hell he'd kept his comments to himself.

The awkward moment passed as they were seated and studied the menu. After making their selection, he went to the counter and ordered for them; steak sandwiches with fries and milkshakes. While they waited for the food to be prepared, he returned to the booth and after making sure they were unobserved, took her hand.

"Joanna, I'd like to ask you something. Whatever your answer, it will be okay by me." He had a lot riding on her answer but he tried to keep it casual.

She met his eyes and waited with a look of apprehension.

"I'd like you to go to Branson with me the weekend after school closes, if you don't have anything planned?"

She gave an audible sigh and smiled. "No, I don't have any other plans. And yes, I'd love to go."

"Great. We can discuss the details later but I just wanted to get your answer before I made a reservation."

They didn't linger over their meal as both were aware of the work waiting for Joanna back in her office. It had grown dark now and they could see only silhouettes with lighted windows towering above them on either side as they walked toward Patterson Hall.

Joanna paused at the steps. "Thanks so much, Pete. This was really sweet of you and I—"

"I'm not going yet." Pete took her arm and

propelled her toward the entrance. "I don't like leaving you in this almost empty building alone to work till God knows when."

"I'll be fine—"

"But I wouldn't be. So I'll just sit in your waiting room and read something while you get on with your grading. Then I'll see you to your car before I leave."

"You could stay over if you like," she said slowly.

He shook his head. "Not tonight. You don't need any distractions and if I stayed, I would certainly be tempted to distract you, my love."

Joanna smiled. "Okay. I will feel better with you on guard outside my door."

Pete settled himself in a chair near a lamp and picked up a periodical from the table. It was *The English Journal* and he checked the index for Joanna's name. He couldn't remember the name of the article she had written and he didn't know the month but it must have been a recent publication from the conversation she'd had with her faculty friends at the Airport Inn that night. This journal was dated Winter so he examined three more before he found one marked Spring. Bingo. And there was her name, Doctor Joanna Flemming, Memphis State U. He turned to the proper page and began to read.

Her knowledge of the subject was impressive, at least to him. He could imagine her speaking the words on the page. The work was informative, but not stuffy. But even more than her command of words, he admired her for the way she was with students. Going the extra mile to help someone like Ted at the expense of her own time and energy. And he was certain that was not an isolated case. Joanna would be there for all her students, taking a special interest in their lives. Did she see them as her surrogate children? The sons and daughters she would never have?

Pete sat staring into space, remembering her

odd reaction to his remarks about the girl they'd passed a while ago. He'd be sure never to risk upsetting her with a reference like that again.

It was getting late and he still had a long drive home. He had been sorely tempted to accept Joanna's invitation to stay over. She hadn't said but the implication was that he would spend the night at her place. But he knew where that would lead and this was not the time nor place to make love to her. He hadn't come here to take advantage of her in a weak moment. When they made love again, he wanted it to be all the things it had not been the first time.

That's why he was taking her to Branson. He had always believed that love and commitment went together and yet he had planned this getaway for the sole purpose of starting an affair. He knew it would change everything yet he was willing to take that risk. He had already concluded that he and Joanna lived in two different worlds, worlds that neither could give up. So an affair seemed the only solution for them to be together.

Exhaustion overtook him, his eyes closed, and he drifted to sleep. He was still in a state of oblivion when Joanna finally recorded the last test score and left her office.

"Pete," she said softly as she laid a gentle hand on his shoulder. "Wake up, guard duty is over for tonight."

He opened his eyes and sat up straighter. "Sorry I went to sleep on the job. We farmer types are early to bed, and—"

Joanna finished with him. "…Early to rise."

He yawned as he stood. "Did you finish the test scores?"

"All done. Now I can devote tomorrow entirely to student appointments."

"I'm sure you are a wonderful advisor. I have it

on good authority from that guy named Ted that you rate very highly when compared with the other faculty members."

Joanna smiled. "I guess I'm just a bleeding heart. But I do try to see things from the students' point of view and bend the rules a little sometimes when the situation requires it."

"I read your article." He gestured toward the journal still open on the seat behind him. "I'm so proud of you, Joanna. That is a very professional piece of writing, in my unprofessional opinion, at least."

"Thank you, Pete." She bent to retrieve her brief case but Pete placed his hands on her shoulders and turned her to face him. Their eyes met for a long moment and she stepped toward him so that their bodies were touching. She lifted her face and his arms went around her, pulling her even closer as their lips met. She felt soft and pliant, molding herself to the hard contours of his lean frame.

When the long kiss ended, she nestled into the hollow of his neck. He brushed a wisp of hair from her cheek and cradled her head against him, planting light kisses along the line of her jaw and the top of her ear.

"Joanna. Joanna." Her name was a soft caress on his tongue and she trembled in his arms. "I've a mind to lock that door and keep you here till morning. But I suppose that would compromise your reputation with the faculty."

"They'd be green with envy." She laughed softly. "Once they recovered from the shock."

"It is I they would envy. You're adorable. Even when you are dead on your feet. But in spite of my strong urge to ravish you, I'm going to see you home. I stayed to defend you, not devour you."

Resolutely, he let her go and picked up her brief case. "Let's get out of here while I still have the will power to do so."

He took her hand, leading her into the dim hallway and out of the building. They walked quickly to the parking lot, the only people visible in the moonlit shadows of the tall oaks.

At her car, they embraced briefly again. "Drive carefully, Joanna. I'll follow you and see that you are safely inside and then be on my way."

"Would you like to come in for coffee before you go? It's so late and I don't want you falling asleep on the drive home."

He hesitated, then shook his head. "You need to get to bed, my love. I'll stop at a fast food drive-in before I leave town."

He took her face in his hands. "Joanna. Take care. I don't want you to be exhausted next weekend when we go to Branson. I want you to enjoy every moment of our time together."

"I will, Pete. I'm looking forward to it."

"I'll call you tomorrow night."

"Thank you, Pete. This was one of the nicest surprises I ever had."

"There'll be more, my darling," Pete promised and their lips met in a final kiss before they said goodbye.

CHAPTER NINE

"Thank God the summer term is finally over. I thought it would never end." Eve swung the Chevy into her space in the parking garage and turned off the ignition.

"There's still commencement," Joanna reminded her as she pulled her brief case from the back seat and opened the car door.

"After struggling with all those classes and putting the exhibit together, it's a mere afterthought." Eve waved her arm in a gesture of dismissal and began gathering her assortment of string bags together, then locked the car. The two women walked toward the entrance of Beekman Place.

"Speaking of the exhibit, how was your dinner date with the lawyer—Mister Averill, wasn't it?" Eve had accepted an invitation to go to dinner with a man who had attended the art exhibit. He had actually invited them both but she had politely declined. The man had been charming and his expensive-looking suit and polished manners had been enough to impress Eve into an eager acceptance.

"Cliff. Oh, it was very nice. He wined and dined me in the elegant style to which I'm sure he is accustomed and then we came to my place and talked for a while." She shrugged as they entered the foyer. “But I never quite got past the feeling I was being cross-examined by the esteemed district attorney. And from his probing questions, he seemed definitely more interested in you than me.”

“He’s a district attorney?” Joanna shifted her briefcase and pushed the elevator button.

“Right, for Shelby County. But enough about him. Have you made any plans for your first week of freedom?”

“Yes, I have,” Joanna answered, “at least, for next weekend. I’m going to Branson with Pete Damron.”

Eve squealed with delight as the elevator door opened. “That’s marvelous. I’m so glad he’s taking you someplace where there’s no family to interfere—his *or* yours,” she added pointedly in reference to that recently aborted evening of seduction she’d encouraged. “A neutral setting, just what you two need. And what could be more romantic than a weekend in the Ozarks? Misty mountains, blue lakes, lively music, and mad, passionate love.”

Eve hugged herself and smiled dreamily. “Take the advice of a good friend, and live a little. We only go around once in this lifetime and it can be a helluva merry-go-round ride if you grab the brass ring and hold on.”

“I’ll think about it.” Joanna returned Eve’s smile as she opened her door. “But I can’t promise anything. I’ve always been the reserved type, you know. It’s not easy to change.”

“But worth the effort, believe me. And for starters, we’ll go shopping downtown for some really sexy lingerie at Cytherea’s Pleasures.”

“I don’t think—” Joanna began but Eve stopped her protest.

“Trust me. The voice of experience has spoken. See you about ten in the morning.”

Joanna unlocked her door and went inside. Eve

had described the situation well. She and Pete did need time together without family interference. But after she had seen the measure of Pete's deep pain she wondered if she would ever be able to help him forget. Still, he had said he was ready to move on so this time alone together would prove it. When she accepted Pete's invitation to Branson, she'd made a decision to follow her heart whatever the consequences.

In spite of her relief that school had ended, Joanna found it difficult to relax. Friday's trip downtown with Eve to enhance her wardrobe only increased her apprehension. They lunched at a health food restaurant and then returned home where she spent the remainder of the day and evening trying various clothes and hairstyles, packing and repacking her bags. Then she gave herself a manicure while resisting the effort to call Pete and say she'd caught a virus and couldn't make it.

The man she would be spending the weekend with was not the boy who had taken her virginity in one unplanned night of passionate goodbyes but she wanted him just as much as she had then. Only she was still the same ingénue while he had years of experience to bring to this reunion of their hearts. She wondered if a purchase from a sexy lingerie shop would be enough to compensate for that.

After a sleepless night, Joanna was waiting just inside the lobby with her luggage when Pete's car turned into the parking lot. Her heartbeat went into overtime as he walked toward the entrance, looking crisp and cool in his black Levi's in spite of the heat rising from the glistening asphalt toward the noonday sun.

She smiled warmly as he approached. "Hello, Pete."

"Hello." His eyes traveled from her freshly

shampooed hair which she had pulled up into a French twist to her floral sundress and lingered on her shapely bare shoulders. "You look terrific."

"So do you." She gestured toward her two small bags. "I thought I'd save time by waiting down here. We can be on our way, unless you'd like something cold to drink?"

"Thanks, I've got a thermos of lemonade in the car. And we'll be stopping soon for lunch, so let's hit the road."

Traffic was heavy as weekenders made their way out of town. They postponed lunch until they crossed the bridge and found a country diner several miles beyond it. They ordered hearty sandwiches but ate little, both too filled with nervous anticipation to be hungry.

Leaving Little Rock and I-40 behind them in mid-afternoon, Pete was driving more slowly now, a concession to the winding curves as they entered the foothills of the Ozarks.

"It's a good thing we stopped back there for lunch." Pete glanced at the desolate countryside, dotted only with an occasional decrepit dwelling. "Because I don't think we're likely to have another chance till we reach Branson."

"I'd forgotten how isolated this part of the country is," Joanna answered. "I haven't been in the Ozarks since our senior trip to Big Springs."

"It was a great trip wasn't it?" Pete said.

She nodded wistfully, remembering with perfect clarity the carefree days she's spent with Pete and the others that final week of high school.

"There are a lot of things to do in Branson. I've got some brochures in the glove compartment. Why don't you get them out and we can discuss what appeals to us."

Joanna took out the brightly-colored folders and studied them. "We may not have time to sleep with all these shows to see."

"We may not have time to sleep, my love, but that is not the reason I have in mind." Pete gave her a measured grin.

She looked at him with an innocent expression. "What do you mean? That's why everyone comes to Branson, isn't it?"

"That's not why I asked *you,* Joanna." He lifted an eyebrow. "Would you like to know my reason or wait and be surprised?"

"Well." She considered his question with mock gravity. "I've always liked surprises. So I suppose I shall have to wait. If it's not too long?"

"It won't be long," he promised.

Joanna looked at Pete's profile as he sat beside her, his strong hands steady on the wheel. It felt so right to be here with this man she had always loved. She leaned back and watched the road as the odometer measured the miles that led them to Branson and the first hours they would ever spend truly alone together.

It was dusk when they pulled under the portico of the hotel. A bellman took their luggage and a valet drove the car away as they entered the lobby. While Pete checked with the registration desk, Joanna looked around her with feigned interest, not really seeing the Victorian sofas and chairs complemented by wallpaper and drapes splashed with pink roses. She felt so fragile that she could imagine shattering into thousands of tiny pieces on the marble floor.

"Come on," he said softly.

They stood almost touching in the compact elevator, and she could feel Pete's breath stirring the wispy tendrils which had escaped from her upswept hair. The door opened and she moved forward as if in a somnambulistic state.

Inside a penthouse suite, the bellman deposited

their luggage, accepted Pete's folded bills and left them alone, facing each other on opposite sides of the closed door.

"It's lovely," Joanna said, indicating the room with its echoing motif of roses.

"It is nice, isn't it? The hotel's fairly new, I think."

He gestured toward the far wall. "There should be quite a view from the balcony. Want to take a look before the darkness settles in?"

Crossing to the wrought-iron railing, Joanna gazed at the sweeping panorama below them. Winding streets where cars, like a string of lightning bugs, crawled slowly along; buildings dotting the steep hills, their lighted windows twinkling in the shadows; and beyond, dark silhouettes of trees that rimmed the hubbub of the tourist town with silent splendor.

Joanna leaned both hands on the railing and took a shallow breath then said in a steady voice, "It *is* quite a view."

Pete stepped closer and placed his hands on either side of hers, touching her ever so slightly, making her aware of his closeness. Joanna shivered with anticipation.

"Cold?" Pete whispered, his lips almost touching her ear.

"No, I—yes." She suddenly felt dizzy and turned away from the precipitous drop. Pete did not move back but enfolded her gently in his arms. For a moment her head rested against his shoulder, then he lifted her chin and bent to touch her lips with his own. At first the kiss was tentative, then with bold and certain motion, his mouth proprietarily possessed hers. He pressed her closer against the lean hardness of his body responding to her nearness. Finally, he pulled away from her and wordlessly led her inside, where in the semi-darkness he slowly removed the pins from her hair and ran his fingers through the loosened strands. He undressed her, then himself and lay with her on the rose-strewn coverlet. With indrawn breath, he gazed at her body for a long moment. Finally he spoke. “It’s hard to believe that the girl who filled all my waking and sleeping dreams in a faraway foxhole so many years ago, is here in this room with me now.”

“I’m here,” she assured him.

He stroked her face, whispered huskily, “I love you, Joanna. I always have, somewhere deep inside my heart. I want you to know that nothing—no one—has ever changed that. Do you believe me?”

“Yes, Pete,” she whispered back, “I believe you because I feel that way, too.”

His gentle hand moved to the valley between her breasts, slowly circling to caress first one, then the other. His breathing grew ragged with his forced restraint and her own came in short gasps as her mounting desire grew almost unbearable.

They kissed deeply, tongues tangling with ever more rapid movement, even as his hands explored her thighs and the recess between. She moaned softly and Pete wrenched his mouth away.

“Joanna.” He spoke through harsh breaths. “I can use protection, but I’ve never been with any woman since my wife.”

“And I’ve never been with any man since you,” she whispered.

“Oh my God, Joanna.” The agonized words tore from his throat. “I don’t know whether to be glad you’ve waited for this, or sorry for all the years of pleasure you’ve missed.”

“After you, I never wanted anyone else,” she told him truthfully.

With a groan, half despair, half ecstasy, he entered her and their bodies melded into one, culminating quickly into climax despite Pete’s efforts to hold back.

"I'm sorry," Pete said softly, "I just couldn't wait. It's been a long time."

"It's all right, Pete," she said as she snuggled against his rapidly beating heart. "Just being close to you is wonderful."

"Let me hold you for a little while, and then I'll make love to you the way I've dreamed of doing so many times." His arm tightened around her and he buried his face in her hair.

She kissed his forehead. "Promise?" she asked lightly.

"Cross my heart and hope to die," he said drowsily and in moments he slept, one arm resting across her breasts, one leg carelessly draped over her thighs. She welcomed the weight of his limp body, happy in the knowledge that she had given him pleasure. The room grew quite dark and only the faint sounds of traffic far below and Pete's even breathing broke the stillness of the night.

Joanna dozed, too, and drifted into dreams of Pete and a warm spring night and a pear tree in bloom. He was kissing her and saying her name and asking her forgiveness and she was crying and murmuring brokenly that she couldn't bear him to leave her. And then she felt his lips on her face and she woke and knew that the dream was reality.

"Joanna. Oh, Joanna." He reached to turn on the bedside lamp but she laid her hand on his arm, not wanting him to see her naked body in the light. He read her wish and whispered, "All right, for now. But later I want to look at you. I want to see you when I make love to you."

His hands roved over her, pleasuring her in places she had never known could bring such heightened desire. Then he caressed her with his lips and tongue until she was writhing with need for release and finally when she arched toward him, he entered her and began moving deep inside until their bodies fused in one giant explosion that rocked the universe and left them clinging wordlessly to each other in its aftermath.

Joanna lay exhausted, still in a state of awe at what she had just felt. It was as though she suddenly realized what it meant to be a woman—a woman fully loved by a man. Now she knew what all the songs were saying, what all the great novels were about, what made lovers smile at each other in that certain way. She felt like crying and laughing and maybe going out onto the balcony and shouting the news to the whole world, "I know. I know."

"Happy?" Pete asked her softly, pushing a wisp of her hair away from her face.

"Happy? It isn't a big enough word to describe what I feel," she told him. "Maybe euphoric. No, more than that. How can I thank you?"

"You just did," he answered huskily before he kissed her again, leisurely moving his mouth over her sensitive lips. Later, he said ruefully, "We haven't had dinner. Are you hungry?"

"No," she said with a contented sigh. "You've just satisfied a hunger I didn't even know I had. And I feel completely sated."

He pulled her to him with a gruff sound. "Joanna, you are the most adorable woman a man could ever have. I didn't think I could love you more, but these few hours have proved me wrong. By morning I may decide to lock the door and throw away the key and keep you here with me forever."

"You'll feel differently in the harsh light of day," she answered sleepily, but at the moment she couldn't remember why she felt so certain that he would.

"Not on your life, my darling," he promised before he too, slept, holding the woman he loved in a fierce embrace.

CHAPTER TEN

Pete awoke when the first streaks of daylight outlined the horizon and lay watching the woman beside him. Joanna stirred and he brushed his lips against her forehead and smoothed her dark hair which fanned across the pillow.

"Good morning, sleepyhead," he whispered.

"Ummm." She slowly opened her eyes, feeling content in the knowledge that she lay against Pete's chest, then she remembered that she had nothing on and reached for the sheet.

Staying her hand, Pete whispered, "No, let me look at you."

Suddenly more concerned with her face which still bore traces of yesterday's makeup than with her less-than-perfect body, she said, "I look terrible in the morning, even after a good night's sleep."

Pete chuckled. "And last night couldn't qualify as one of those."

"I'm not complaining," said Joanna.

"You could never look anything but wonderful to me," he assured her as his hand stroked her back in lazy circles. Then with a sudden surge of passion, he pulled her closer so that she felt his arousal and began touching her in ways that ignited her own desire.

"Joanna, you make me feel as if I could make love to you for days and never stop," he mumbled huskily.

"No one is asking you to stop," she whispered, and he held her even closer, kissing her with all the longing he had subconsciously repressed through so many years without her.

They made love again slowly, touching, tasting, tantalizing each other with new sensations as they explored the seemingly limitless expression of their feelings. Murmuring soft words of endearment, they crossed the barriers of time and distance that had separated them and joined together to reach new heights of pleasure that left them awed anew.

Afterward they lay together in a suspended state of bliss for a while, then Pete broke the spell. "Would you like to go out for breakfast or shall we order room service, my love?"

"Either way," Joanna answered. "I have no preference."

"Then let's eat out and explore the town," said Pete. "I need a hearty meal or else I won't have the stamina for other activities I hope to continue later on." He grinned meaningfully at her. "I'm not as young as I used to be, in spite of the way you make me feel."

"Oh?" Joanna gave him a coy smile. "You had me fooled."

"Go take your shower." He gave her a gentle nudge. "And lock the door in case I get an uncontrollable desire to join you and postpone going out indefinitely."

"An interesting possibility." Joanna pretended to give his words serious thought as she got out of bed. "Perhaps we might consider it."

"Later, after I get my strength back," Pete promised her and she wasn't sure whether he was teasing or tempting her with unexplored pleasures yet to come.

It was only in the shower that she finally

remembered the expensive lingerie from Cytherea's Pleasures, still lying folded in her luggage.

They walked next door to the Grand Village—a collection of shops and restaurants clustered about an open courtyard—and chose for breakfast a quaint place called the Hard Luck Diner with its fittingly nostalgic 1950's decor and menu. Sitting at a glass and wrought iron table on the patio, Joanna breathed the crisp mountain air, redolent with the aroma of fresh-brewed coffee, with a heightened sense of awareness. Sunlight washed the multi-hued beds of flowers with brilliant color and without touching them she could feel their velvet petals, taste their nectar. The sounds from a nearby fountain had the intensity of a thundering waterfall, yet each drop of spray separately distinct.

I am drowning in psychedelic sensations, Joanna marveled, feeling more alive than she could ever remember. She wondered if Pete felt that way too, and might have asked him, but while she was trying to think how to describe it with words, the waitress brought their food and the question was forgotten.

After they had eaten, they lingered over coffee, smiling and holding hands like honeymooners; then strolled into the cobblestone courtyard and window shopped until the display in a store called Bear Hollow caught their attention.

"Come on, let's go inside." Pete guided her into the shop where the walls were lined with hundreds of stuffed animals in every size and color imaginable. "Help me choose a bear for Robin," Pete said. "What do you think she would like?"

Joanna wandered among the furry bruins, finally stopping to hold a particularly winsome specimen. "I can't really say which Robin would like best, but this one appeals to me." Its silky fur was the color of wild honey and a blue taffeta bow was bunched at its chubby neck. "Look at those eyes." Joanna turned the bear to face Pete. "Can you resist that 'Take me home with you' message?"

Pete chuckled. "Not for a moment, especially with you pleading its cause so eloquently." He took the bear from her. "Shall I ask the saleslady to wrap it or would you like to cuddle it the rest of the day?"

"You'd better have him wrapped before I become so attached to this fella I don't want to give him up."

Farther on they paused to look at a window display of western wear and Joanna said, "I'd like to go in here and look for a gift for Eve. She's watering my plants while I'm away."

"Take your time," Pete told her, "I'll be across the way at T. Charleston's, browsing through the books."

Joanna quickly found a denim vest with spangles and fringe that she knew Eve would be ecstatic over.

"Could I show you a skirt and blouse to go with that?" the young salesclerk asked.

"Oh, this is not for me."

"You'd look great in one of these faded denim skirts. And we have shirts to match. Want to try them on?"

"Well..." Joanna looked doubtful, then smiled as she took the items the clerk had selected for her. "Why not?"

A short while later, Joanna left the store carrying a shopping bag containing the clothes she had worn in, and headed for the book store. I feel like a different person inside so I may as well change the outside image, she told herself and wondered belatedly if Pete would like her metamorphosis. She didn't have to wait long for her answer.

"Wow," Pete said when she was close enough to hear him. "You look great in that outfit."

"When in Rome..." Joanna smiled and shrugged.

Her new look was definitely more correlated with Pete's casual jeans and the Branson country music image.

"Will you excuse me for a minute?" Pete asked, "I've just thought of something else I want to buy."

"Of course. I saw another interesting shop I'd like to check. I want to buy a gift for Betsy. Let's meet at the fountain."

"Half an hour?"

Joanna nodded, watched Pete walk away, then picked up the book of contemporary poetry he had put down and took it to the register. She'd debated what to get for him and he had just given her the answer.

The sun was growing hotter and the fine spray from the fountain felt good on Joanna's arms as she waited for Pete.

"All set?" He took her hand and she tingled at his touch. "How about a cup of cappuccino and a croissant at the Village Cafe before we go back to the hotel?"

She nodded.

"I have to supplement my energy level with carbs and caffeine for what I have planned," he added meaningfully and Joanna met his eyes with an intimate smile.

After they had ordered, Pete laid a gift-wrapped package on the table. "For you, Joanna."

She took the small box, removed the silver paper, then lifted its lid and gasped in surprise. "Oh, Pete, how lovely."

"I thought you needed this to wear with your new clothes," Pete explained.

"It's perfect. Thank you." She held the turquoise bracelet out to him. "Will you fasten it on, please?"

"Look inside first."

She turned the bracelet over, read the inscription. It simply said "Pete loves Joanna" followed by yesterday's date and the place. Joanna looked down to hide her expression, afraid Pete would see the secrets hidden in her heart. She felt emotions welling for all that was gone and all that might still be lost. The bracelet said everything and Joanna's eyes filled with happy tears as Pete fastened the silver clasp on her wrist, then raised her hand and kissed her open palm.

****

Joanna glanced at her watch as she hurried to answer the doorbell, certain it could only be her next-door neighbor this early in the morning.

"I hope I didn't wake you?" Eve stood in the hallway wearing faded jeans and a halter top, her long hair in braids.

Joanna smiled, shook her head. "Come in."

"Thanks, but I'm on my way downtown. The Smokers Rights group is having a parade, then a rally at Overton Park this afternoon, so GASP—that's our Group Against Smokers Pollution—is going to do likewise. I stopped to see if you'd like to join us."

"Sorry, I can't. I'm packing for a trip to Greenville."

"Well, hey, that's okay. The crops all gathered in?"

"Yes, Pete called last night. Thank goodness the rain held off until they finished combining."

"You're beginning to sound like a farm wife." Eve looked at her intently. "But somehow I just can't picture you in a rural setting."

"I love farm life," Joanna said quietly.

"Then go for it," Eve said emphatically. "By the way, did you check your horoscope today?"

Joanna shook her head and Eve went on. "There's romance in the forecast for you. Either Leo or Capricorn involved. What was Pete's sign again?"

"You *know* he's Capricorn, but thanks for the

prediction."

"Don't thank me, thank the stars. Well, gotta go now. Have a fabulous weekend."

"You, too, Eve. And do be careful."

"I'll try, but there are a lot of loonies in that smokers group."

Joanna smiled as she closed the door. Eve Whitfield was always involved in some controversial issue. Joanna was glad she had a legitimate excuse not to join in today because she really wasn't comfortable carrying placards in public places. But she didn't have time to think about marches. She'd told Pete she would be there before noon.

At the thought of Pete, she felt a warmth suffuse her body. It had been almost two weeks since she had seen him, although he had phoned every night. She longed to be in Pete's arms and from his phone conversations she thought he was as eager as she to make love again. Still, she knew it would seem strange to sleep with Pete in Mary Esther's house, in Mary Esther's bed. As she closed her luggage, she reminded herself that the house and bed belonged exclusively to Pete now and resolved to banish the ghost of Mary Esther from her mind.

When Joanna arrived at the farm, Pete greeted her as if they had been separated far longer than a couple of weeks. Wrapping his arms tightly around her, he murmured into her ear, "Ah, Joanna, I've missed you. And I plan to show you just how much as soon as I feed you lunch."

"I've missed you, too," Joanna whispered and raised her face to meet his mouth as it closed over hers.

The kiss was slow and sensuous and left them both shaken when they pulled apart.

"Lunch first," Pete admonished himself.

"I *am* hungry," Joanna admitted, "or I'd challenge that."

They linked arms and walked toward the house, then Pete stopped. “I guess I'd better get your bags and put your car in the garage now.”

“To protect my reputation or yours?” Joanna teased.

“Both,” he answered grimly. “I seem to be the focus of a smear campaign already.”

“Oh, Pete, maybe I shouldn't have—”

“It's all right, Joanna. What we do is really nobody's business but ours. I just don't want to add any fuel to the fire. Now don't look so solemn. I've made you a great lunch of barbequed chicken and vegetables from the garden and Bets sent over a fresh peach pie.”

Joanna gave him a wry smile. “So Betsy approves of us?”

“You bet. And she said to come by and say hello if you had time.” He grinned meaningfully. “But I told her you wouldn't have time.”

Pete brought her two small bags inside and led the way to the bedroom wing on the opposite side of the house from the master suite. Joanna gave a grateful sigh that he had understood her unspoken feelings.

They spent the afternoon in bed, finally breaking their romantic interlude to fortify themselves with food. When darkness fell, they went out to the pool and began what they had left unfinished a night there not so long ago.

“Ummm, this is even nicer than making love in a shower,” Joanna whispered against Pete's ear as the warm water undulated around their joined bodies in the moonlit pool.

“And the night has just begun.” Pete nuzzled her neck. “We still haven't made love in the hammock under the oaks, or—”

Joanna put her fingers to his lips to stop his words. “No, don't tell me. Surprise me.”

Pete caught her hand, gently nibbled at her fingertips, then his tongue made a sinuous trail across her palm and wrist. She shivered with pleasure and met his lips in a long, deep kiss.

"Dad? Anybody home?"

"I'm in the pool, Rebecca," he called as he scrambled out of the water and grabbed his trunks. "Go on inside and I'll be right there."

"Shall I stay here?" Joanna whispered.

"No, come on in." He wrapped a towel around his trim waist and headed toward the house.

"My clothes are inside," Joanna said more loudly as she heard the front door close and knew that Rebecca had gone into the house.

Pete stopped, momentarily nonplussed, then said, "There's a robe in the shower room. Just wear that." He assumed a casual air and strolled toward the den where lights now blazed.

"What brings you out so late tonight, Becky?"

Ignoring his question, his stern-faced daughter said, "I didn't know you had company." She nodded toward Joanna's clothes strewn across the floor, a pair of black lace panties and bra clearly visible near the glass patio door.

Pete's face flushed. He cleared his throat. "Yes, well, not really company. Joanna is here for the weekend."

As if his words had conjured up her presence, Joanna spoke from directly behind him with as much aplomb as she could muster. "Hello, Rebecca."

Rebecca mumbled hello and returned her attention to Pete. "My classes are larger this year and I really need another sewing machine and stove. And they should be ordered right away so I'd like to bypass regular procedure with a special request."

"I'm sure we could consider that."

"Fine. I'll be going then and let you get back to...your swim." She wheeled around and walked toward the front door without saying another word.

"Becky, wait, won't you—" Pete called after her but the front door slammed before he could get the words out of his mouth.

"I'm sorry, Pete," Joanna said as she stooped to gather up her clothes, wishing she'd never heard of Cytherea's Pleasures.

"Hey, there's nothing to be sorry for." Pete crossed the room to help her. "I'm the one who needs to apologize. I should have taught my kids better manners."

He reached out a hand to her. "Come here, Joanna, and sit beside me. The night is young yet." He held her close against him, chucked his hand under her chin, lifted her face and kissed each eyelid. "I want to finish what we started a moment ago. Now where were we before we were so rudely interrupted?"

"Please lock the door first." Joanna cautioned him with a wry smile. "I've had quite enough surprises for one night."

Pete chuckled. "You get the lights and I'll lock the door, but I won't promise no more surprises tonight. You bring out the urge to use all of my inventive powers."

"Don't you ever get tired?" Joanna chided as Pete stood, and pulled her up.

"No, Joanna, I could make love with you forever. I've waited almost that long to begin."

CHAPTER ELEVEN

Joanna woke at dawn with Pete's warm breath against her cheek.

"Is it morning already?" she mumbled without opening her eyes.

"It is, and I love to look at you when I wake up," he said softly and pushed a strand of her hair away from her forehead, then gently stroked her face. "You have fulfilled my every need yet I know I will always want more of you. You were my first love but what we have this second time around is even better."

"Yes," she agreed and snuggled closer.

"You're still half asleep so I'm going to shower now but I'll be back soon," he promised as he gently disentangled himself from her embrace.

She was vaguely aware when Pete crept out of bed and went across the house toward the master suite to use his shower, leaving the adjoining bath for her. They had slept in the guest room with space to spare on the double bed. In truth, they would have been comfortable sleeping on a twin bed since Pete had held her all night long. She wondered what Pete's thoughts were as he passed the king-size bed with Mary Ester's picture on the table beside it. Perhaps he has put the picture away, she thought, before she dozed again.

"Wake up, sleepyhead." Pete kissed the top of

her nose, and her even breathing became fainter. "You're on a farm this morning. It's time to rise and shine."

"Already?" Joanna opened one eye and saw Pete sitting beside her. He wore a faded pair of jeans with nothing above and she reached to stroke the damp hair on his bare chest.

"Already." He confirmed and took her hand, held it to his mouth and kissed it softly. "The chef is here to take your order for breakfast. Will it be bacon and eggs, waffles, omelets, juice, coffee, or all of the above?"

"Ummmm. surprise me." She answered sleepily.

"Again?" Pete laughed softly. "Okay, you just take your shower while I rustle up another great surprise. Don't be too long." He patted her bare bottom and said huskily, "I'll get started on breakfast now before my will power gives way."

She lay relaxed for a few blissful moments longer, then the aroma of perking coffee coaxed her to sit up. Just as she reached for her robe, she heard the door chimes ring.

Who could that be so early? Surely not Rebecca again...

She heard the door open, then Pete's hearty voice from the hallway.

"Well look who's here. Two of my favorite girls."

"Hi, Gwampie."

"Don't you look pretty this morning. Have you got a kiss for your Grampie?"

Oh, no, first Rebecca and now LaWanda. What had she done to deserve this?

"Kiss Pooh," Robin said.

"Oh, Grampie forgot. Sorry."

After a moment Pete spoke again. "Come on in LaWanda, if it won't make you late for Mass."

"Just for a minute." She heard LaWanda answer. "Come on, Robin."

The voices got louder as Pete led the way down the hall to the kitchen. "I was just making waffles. Would you—"

"Cook, Gwampie?"

"Yes, Robin, I—"

She heard LaWanda's strident tone as she interrupted Pete's words. "Dad, can we talk?"

This was no social call, Joanna quickly surmised. But what to do? Make her presence known as soon as possible, she decided. She grabbed her clothes from the chair and make a hasty retreat to the bathroom to dress and repair her makeup.

In seconds, Joanna was back in the bedroom, where she could hear the conversation which had grown more heated.

".. .but I just couldn't believe you would do this to our mother." LaWanda's voice sounded near tears.

"This has nothing to do with your mother. Joanna and I—" Pete began but his daughter cut off his protest.

"Really, Dad, what I find hardest of all to take is your bringing that...woman here to sleep in our mother's bed. How could you?"

She cringed as Pete thundered, "For your information, Joanna has never slept in your mother's bed. Though it is no longer her bed anyway. And let me remind you that both you and your sister have barged in here uninvited and unannounced!"

"Since when do we have to be invited to come to our mother's house?" LaWanda choked out the words and Joanna felt her pain.

"LaWanda, let me repeat." Pete spoke in a measured tone. "This is no longer your mother's house. Your mother is dead. Has been for over three years now."

LaWanda's voice caught on a sob and Joanna put her hand over her mouth, torn between rushing to reassure her and sobbing herself. Finally she said in a subdued voice, "I never thought you'd act like this, Daddy. I thought you loved our mother."

Now she wanted to rush to Pete's side and reassure his daughter that he did but Pete's next words proved that he was able to defend himself against the unjust accusation.

"My God, LaWanda," Pete exploded. "I did love your mother, do love her. At least, I love her memory. But I'm not married to a memory. I'm human. And I have needs—physical and emotional needs—that a dead woman can't satisfy."

"Oh, Daddy, how can you even think about sleeping with anyone else...especially a woman like Joanna Flemming?"

Joanna clenched her fists. Now she'd like to shake the girl and she just might do that if Pete didn't do it for her.

"What's wrong with Joanna?" Pete demanded.

"Everything. She's not Catholic. She's not one of us. She just doesn't fit into the family, not like Betsy would."

"Betsy? Why, Betsy's like a member of the family already."

"Exactly, and *Doctor* Flemming never will be."

Joanna took a deep breath. This had gone far enough. Time to face the little hellion and try to sort things out. With grim determination she strode down the hall, pausing in the doorway to force a friendly smile.

"Hello, LaWanda." She looked at Pete and her smile was genuine. "Mmmm, smells delicious. Are the waffles ready?"

Without waiting for his answer, she turned toward LaWanda and added, "I hope you're staying for breakfast?"

"Where's Robin?" Pete asked before LaWanda could respond.

"Robin?"

"Yes, we thought she was with you." Pete took a step toward the hallway from which Joanna had come. "Didn't you see her?"

"No." Joanna shook her head, looking worried. "Was she supposed to be with me?" Pete was already out of range of her question, calling the little girl as he went from room to room.

"Yes, when Dad said you were here she went to find you." LaWanda shot her an accusing glare, then she raised her voice sternly. "Robin, don't play hide-and-seek. Come out wherever you are. It's time to go." She followed Pete from the kitchen without another look.

Joanna stood for a moment, brows knit together, the overheard conversation between Pete and his daughter still stinging in her ears. But she would deal with that later; right now they needed to find Robin. Since both Pete and LaWanda had gone toward the bedroom wing, she would check the den; perhaps the little girl was watching the television which Pete had taught her how to operate. The lack of sound told her the answer even before she saw the blank screen and empty sofa. But as she glanced around the room, now in perfect order with no trace of last night's activities, she saw one sliding glass door was slightly open and a chill of apprehension shot up her spine.

Quickly she crossed the room, opened the door wider, and stepped onto the patio. Her eyes swept the area around the pool and froze with fear on the honey-colored bear floating on the water. Her throat constricted and she opened her mouth and tried to scream for Pete but the sound was only a strangled croak. Running, she jumped into the pool and, taking a deep breath, dived below the surface, frantically searching for something solid with her hands but finding nothing. She willed herself to open her eyes and the chlorine stung for a moment; then she could see, but there was only the murky water, nothing else.

When her lungs felt ready to explode, she broke the water, took another deep breath and went under again. She enlarged the area of her search, circling farther away from the floating bear. This time her foot touched something solid and she rose again and filled her lungs with air before she dived lower to grasp and bring Robin's limp body to the surface.

"Pete! Pete, come quick!" she screamed as she hauled the child out of the pool and placed her gently on the flagstone at its edge. She bent her ear to Robin's chest. Nothing. She grabbed a small wrist, felt for a pulse. Nothing. "Pete! Pete!" she screamed again, just as he burst through the door.

"Joanna, what...Oh my God." He strode across the patio, knelt and checked the still form for signs of life and finding none, raised desperate eyes to Joanna. "She's...quick, call an ambulance. No, it will take too long for—"

"Dad, what's all the..." LaWanda appeared in the doorway, saw the two figures bent above her child and screamed. "Robin!"

She ran to them, began flailing her arms in a frantic effort to tear Joanna away from her position astride the little girl's prone body where she had begun resuscitation attempts.

"Stop it, LaWanda." Pete's tone brought the frightened mother's screams and useless movements to a sudden halt. "Call an ambulance. Tell them to meet us. We'll be in the truck on 71 to Cape. Describe it. Hurry!"

Joanna tilted the child's chin back, made an attempt to open her air passageway. There was no response. *Oh God, help me remember what to do.* She bent closer, placed her mouth over Robin's mouth and nose and blew two consecutive breaths. She waited. Nothing. She breathed into the child again.

Waited. Again. She looked at Pete. "I've got to do CPR," she said.

"Do you know—"

She didn't let him finish. "Yes."

He stood up. "I'll get the keys and start the truck, then I'll be back for you."

Joanna placed her hand flat on Robin's chest, her other hand above it and pressed. Waited. Pressed again. Wait. Press. Wait. Press. She counted, and at the proper interval she forced breath into the lungs. Where was Pete? What was taking so long? Suddenly, strong arms were moving her aside, lifting Robin, and running toward the truck parked just outside the fence. A quilt lay on the flat bed and she followed and crawled into position and resumed her ministrations, barely aware of his words.

"I'll try to drive carefully. LaWanda will be with you. If you want me to stop, tell her and she can beat on the back glass."

Joanna looked up briefly and saw the child's mother crouched in a sitting position, whimpering, and saying her rosary.

"Hail, Mary, Mother of God."

Joanna nodded and continued counting, pressing, blowing, waiting. The truck eased out of the driveway and they were on the open road, the sun hot on her back. Sweat ran down her face but she didn't stop to wipe it away. She was tired, so tired. Her breath came in measured gasps, dredged from an unconscious source of power. Finally, a strangled sound, then mucus and water erupted from Robin's slack mouth. She jerked the child's head sideways, ran a finger into her mouth in an attempt to clear the remaining fluid away, listened for and heard a faint heartbeat. Then nothing. Faintly, once again. Tilting Robin's head back, she closed her mouth over the foul-smelling foam that dribbled from the child's lips and nose and blew into her lungs with renewed vigor. *Dear God, please.* Blow gently. Press. Wait. Stop. Bend an ear to listen. Thump...Thump...Thump...

Joanna lifted her head, met LaWanda's pleading look and nodded. Disbelief seemed to fight with the desire to believe what she was being told, then a sob of evident relief and gratitude tore from her throat.

In the distance, Joanna became aware of the faint wail of a siren. As she intently watched the irregular rising and falling of the child's chest, monitored her ragged breaths, the sound came closer. Finally, Pete pulled to the side of the road and the paramedics leaped onto the truck and secured Robin to the stretcher. LaWanda tried to follow as they lifted her child into the waiting ambulance but Pete held her back.

"No, you'll be in their way. Come on, get in the cab of the truck. We'll be right behind them."

Joanna took LaWanda's arm, led her quickly to the passenger side, pushed her in, and climbed in beside her. Pete drove over the speed limit, staying in sight of the wailing vehicle ahead of them. In the small enclosure, no one spoke, but LaWanda reached for Joanna's hand and held on as if she herself were drowning.

At the emergency entrance to the hospital, the ambulance had already unloaded its passengers, and Pete wheeled in beside it, running to catch up with them, leaving Joanna to follow with a dazed LaWanda. Inside, people rushed back and forth, calling orders, paying no attention to Pete's questions or the two women huddled together at one side of the entrance.

The paramedics stopped beside them as they were leaving.

"If you hadn't done CPR, the little girl wouldn't have made it for sure."

The taller man shook his head, looked at

Joanna. "She has a good chance now, thanks to you."

Joanna nodded and the two men left.

LaWanda looked at her solemnly, then said in a contrite voice, "Can you ever forgive me?"

Joanna placed an arm around the younger woman. "There's nothing to forgive."

"But you don't understand. I had come to tell Dad how angry I was that you were there and—"

"Shhh." Joanna's arm tightened reassuringly. "It's okay. I understand how you feel and I—"

"Why, you're freezing." LaWanda looked at her with concern. "And no wonder, standing here in this air-conditioned room in your wet clothes."

Joanna crossed her arms and clenched her teeth to stop them chattering. She was trembling but she wasn't sure if it was from the cold temperature or finally realizing the full impact of what had happened.

"I'll get someone to find dry clothes you can put on," LaWanda said and started toward the nurses' station. "There has to be an extra set of scrubs lying around—"

Suddenly Pete's voice superimposed itself above what she was saying. "They've suctioned out Robin's lungs. And her heartbeat is steady. They'll watch her for a while but the doctor says she's going to be all right. But if you hadn't..." He looked into Joanna's eyes and his voice choked so that he couldn't go on.

He reached an arm to encompass both women, tears streaming down his face.

Joanna closed her brimming eyes. *Thank You, God.*

"Oh, Daddy." LaWanda broke into happy sobs, then turned to Joanna. "There is no way I can ever thank you for giving my little girl back to me."

Joanna wiped her tears with the back of her hand, and embraced Pete's daughter as though she were her own.

And right at this moment she felt as if she were a part of Pete's family, knowing she had earned the right to be.

CHAPTER TWELVE

The kitchen was redolent with mingled spices and Joanna hummed happily as she chopped broccoli on the cutting board. On the counter nearby lay her carefully planned menu, along with the sequential steps for executing it. She glanced at it once more as she worked, mentally checking off each item.

The turkey was baking in the oven, enveloped in its brown- and-serve bag to preserve its juices for dressing. In a large bowl the cornbread and biscuits were already crumbled, waiting to be combined with chopped celery and onions that simmered on the stove top. The bread wasn't exactly homemade but she had thrown away the cornbread boxes and biscuit cans and no one need be the wiser. Cranberry salad, made last night, chilled in the refrigerator as well as deviled eggs and sliced ham. Candied yams baked alongside the turkey and pans of vegetables waited in various stages of preparation to be finished according to plan. And pumpkin and pecan pies, resplendent in their homemade crusts—courtesy of Betsy's freezer—cooled on the counter.

It was Bets who had helped her plan a menu and furnished the recipes for favorite dishes of Pete and his family. Eve had offered suggestions, too, but considering her penchant for exotic health foods, she had politely declined. Joanna still wasn't sure Pete had liked the meal Eve helped her prepare in her apartment weeks before.

She finished her task and placed the broccoli in a steamer and turned on the burner. Now she would check her recipe and make the white sauce to pour over it at the proper time. But first she walked to the back door and stepped out of the steamy kitchen for a breath of fresh air.

The sky was gray and leaden, hinting of snow, and a chill wind rustled the remaining brown leaves that clung to almost-bare branches on the trees that surrounded the house. She wondered if Pete had dressed warmly enough this morning when he had gone with Kyle and his two sons-in-law duck hunting. Richard had missed this holiday tradition since he and Ivana had volunteered to drive to St. Louis to meet Michael's plane. Rebecca was at the school helping her students finish a float they were making for the Christmas parade in Cape tomorrow and LaWanda and Ursula were minding all the children and would be along later.

"Now I know how it feels to be a mother with a large family," Joanna said to herself, and added with a sense of guilt, "even if it is another woman's family." But as she had reminded herself so often these past few months, Mary Esther was gone and surely she'd want someone to love Pete and her children since she was no longer here.

Joanna returned to the kitchen and measured flour and butter into a saucepan, stirring as the mixture heated. Only it wasn't a mixture, just glue-like white blobs sliding around in rapidly browning yellow liquid. She turned the burner lower, poured in a generous measure of milk and stirred vigorously but the lumps remained. After cooking a bit longer, the sauce still appeared to be a little thin so Joanna cautiously sprinkled in additional flour. That seemed to help, and she repeated the same amount. The sauce was beginning to look too thick again so she added more butter. She probably should have doubled the recipe since what is in the saucepan doesn't look like nearly enough to cover the large amount of broccoli being prepared.

Joanna was so engrossed in the process of making white sauce that she didn't notice the smell of scorching celery and onions until it was too late to salvage them.

"Oh, no," she wailed aloud, "now what am I going to do?" She knew there were more onions but she had used all of the celery Pete had in the crisper. Lifting the lid of the steamer, she discovered that the broccoli had overcooked, turning from a deep green to an unappetizing chartreuse.

"Well, the white sauce will cover that problem," she said under her breath. "Better check the turkey. If the bird is a success, I'll probably be forgiven for other minor infractions against tradition."

The turkey had gotten much browner since she had last checked it and she decided it probably didn't need to cook as long as the directions had said. She took two potholders and lifted the pan from the oven and attempted to set it on the counter. One of the hot pads slipped and the pan tilted. The heavy turkey, unbalanced in the shifting, flopped out of the pan and landed on the floor, splitting its air-filled bag and spilling hot juices on the tile.

Joanna, who true to her proper upbringing had always found something other than swear words to express her feelings, swore loudly, using words she wasn't even aware she knew. She stood transfixed, watching in horror as the brown bubbling liquid oozed slowly over the floor, nearer and nearer to her feet. Finally she went into action, grabbing a roll of paper towels from underneath the cabinet and blotting with a vengeance, while the bird lay on the tile, ensconced in its plastic wrapping, drained now of all its succulent drippings.

The unfortunate fowl was still too hot to move and she eyed it with trepidation, imagining what would happen if someone should walk in the back door. Wildly, she cast about for something large enough to hold the thing and finally settled on the cutting board. She wrestled the bird onto the flat surface, and managed to lift it back onto the counter. She wet towels and sopped up more juice, muttering under her breath as she did.

"What am I going to do?" she moaned. She could ask LaWanda and Ursula to come and help. But even though Pete's family had accepted her since the day she had saved Robin, she didn't want to give them any further reason to compare her unfavorably with their mother. She could call Eve to come early, but Eve knew nothing about making traditional Southern meals. Betsy. But she was surely at her son's house in Cape by now. Well, just on the chance she hadn't left, she would try her number.

She dialed the phone and on the second ring, Betsy said hello.

"Thank God I caught you."

"Joanna? Is that you?"

"Yes." Joanna closed her eyes and leaned weakly against the counter. "You won't believe what has happened."

"What is it Joanna?" Betsy asked in an alarmed voice.

"The turkey. The plastic bag split when I was taking it out of the oven and I lost all of the juices and—"

Betsy's relieved laugh interrupted her words. "Is that all? I was afraid something had happened to one of the hunt—never mind. I'm sure everything will be all right."

"But how can I make dressing with no broth? And anyway, I've burned the celery and onions and I don't have any more celery to cook."

"Sounds like you could use some help. Is anyone there with you?"

"Not at the moment. Did you mean that about help? Aren't you supposed to be going to Cape?"

"Already been. We had dinner early so the twins could get back to St. Louis before dark, and so the in-laws could spend time with their families, too. Anyway, I was ready to come home. This holiday was too close to the anniversary of Walt's funeral to be any fun for me." Betsy's voice became matter-of-fact. "Is the bird okay?"

"Yes, still wrapped in plastic."

"Good. Now, I'll bring celery. And some cans of turkey broth just in case Pete doesn't have any on hand. Meanwhile, you chop more onions, and boil eggs for the giblet gravy."

"Oh, Betsy, you just saved the day."

"Well, not yet, but I think it is definitely salvageable. Just hold on, I'll be there in a sec."

Suddenly remembering her other culinary disaster, Joanna added, "Betsy, can you make white sauce?"

"Well, sure. Anybody can make white sauce, Joanna."

"Almost anybody," Joanna told her and hung up the phone.

Joanna dumped the scorched celery and onions in the garbage along with the grease-soaked paper towels. She eyed the cooling turkey with reluctant admiration. It was nice and brown and it did smell delicious. She stirred the hopelessly congealed white sauce, then added it to the garbage and washed the pans. The kitchen now showed no evidence of the havoc she had wrought and as she surveyed it wryly, she wondered if Mary Esther had ever felt inadequate to the task of preparing a holiday meal.

"I'm doing the best I can," she said to the empty room. "It is the thought that counts, isn't it?"

Suddenly realizing that she had been talking to herself all day, Joanna refrained from answering yes and proving beyond all doubt that she had gone around the bend. Resolutely, she checked her list again and began to peel more onions just as she heard Betsy's car in the drive. Joanna flung open the back door with a welcome smile. "Oh, Bets, am I glad to see you. What a mess I've made of dinner."

"Not to worry. Everything will be okay. Just give me a minute to sort things out." Joanna took the bag Betsy carried and she shrugged out of her coat.

Soon they were busy cutting, stirring, and tasting and Joanna lost her feeling of panic. "You make it all look so easy, Bets."

"I've had a lot of practice. Husbands and kids require care and feeding, you know."

"I think I'm just beginning to realize that." Her mouth quirked. "Being an only child and then living alone hasn't given me any experience along those lines."

"You'll learn. When you and Pete..." Betsy stopped, then mumbled, "What I mean is, if, ah..." She stopped, took a breath, and started over. "I guess I'm speaking out of turn, but ever since you and Pete went to Branson we have been expecting you to make an announcement any day now."

Joanna shook her head, remembering her conversation with her friends when they'd had lunch a few days before. "I'm still surprised that Vada and Thel knew about that."

Betsy smiled. "Why, people in Greenville probably knew about it before you left. It's a small town. Everyone knows everything."

"Do you suppose they know when I come to stay on weekends?"

"You can count on it."

"Oh, dear, I hadn't really thought it would matter except to Pete's children. Do you suppose people are saying bad things about Pete and—"

"I've heard some talk," Betsy admitted, "but most people think you two will be getting married and of course, that would make things okay."

"But we're not." Joanna felt color rise in her face. "I hope it won't change your opinion of me, Bets, but we're just happy being together. There's nothing more than that, and maybe never will be."

"Do you want more, Joanna?" Betsy asked quietly.

Joanna almost answered yes before she remembered that she could never marry Pete even if he asked her. Instead, she tried to justify the status quo. "I have my job at the university and Pete has the farm, so I don't see how marriage could ever work for us."

"Pete couldn't farm in Memphis, that's for sure. But there are teaching positions around here." She looked thoughtful. "Though perhaps none that you'd care to consider."

Joanna met her best friend's questioning gaze and shook her head. "Pete and I are just friends, Betsy." She glanced toward the clock and changed the subject. "Is it time to bake the dressing now?"

"My goodness, yes. I got to meddling and forgot all about it."

The door chimes rang as Betsy carefully placed the huge casserole dish in the oven.

"That must be Eve and Cliff."

"Oh, I didn't know they would be here."

"Eve said Cliff's daughter was on a cruise so I invited them to share our day. She seems quite serious about him."

Joanna welcomed them at the front door, with Betsy just behind her. Cliff was introduced, then Eve turned toward Betsy.

"Betsy! What fun. I didn't know you were coming."

"Well, I had an early meal with my family and—" She met Joanna's eyes and the two women smiled. "—then Joanna invited me to come over here and pig out again."

"Speaking of pigs," Eve said as she gave a casserole dish to Betsy and Joanna took the string bag and two bottles of wine from Cliff, "I want to see them, and the chickens and cows and everything. May we?"

"Of course." Joanna smiled. "I'm sure Pete would love to conduct a tour for you as soon as he gets back from hunting."

"That may be a while," Betsy told her. "Why don't you take them on out back and I'll finish up dinner. There's not much left to do."

"Well, if you're sure..." Joanna hesitated, then seeing Eve's expectant face, led the way through the kitchen to the back door.

Cliff glanced toward the large covered pool. "Nice place. All the comforts of city living. With considerable acreage besides, from what I've seen."

"Yes," Joanna told him. "Pete has about six thousand acres counting the land his son farms."

Eve took a deep breath as they neared the gate that led to the stables and adjacent hog pens. "Isn't this wonderful? I'd almost forgotten the smell of live animals—oh, Cliff, look at those gorgeous pigs." She ran toward the pen, loose hair blowing in the wind.

Looking toward her instead of the ground as he followed, Cliff stepped in a soft cow pie and cursed aloud, causing the two women to turn toward him. With one polished Gucci loafer oozing odoriferous dung he stood paralyzed with a pained expression on his handsome face.

Eve laughed aloud. "Oh, poor darling. It's easy to see you aren't accustomed to farm life. Just shake your foot a bit and give it a twist or two and you'll never know the difference."

Cliff shrugged and did as directed, then joined the two women to admire the porcine specimens whose smell overshadowed the stuff on his shoe.

"Here's Pete now." Joanna turned toward the house and waved as the tall man strode toward them.

"Sorry I wasn't here to welcome you," Pete said to Cliff and Eve as he approached. "Time gets away when you're bagging lots of birds."

Joanna made the introductions and the two men shook hands eyeing each other with frank appraisal.

"Nice place you have here," Cliff said. "What's your main crop?"

"Alfalfa, soy beans. And we're getting back into growing cotton again since we have new seeds that are more resistant."

Cliff looked puzzled and Pete went on explaining, "The herbicides made the crops later so the cold weather hindered their development and—"

"Dad." A tall blond man in a clerical collar came toward them from the house and the five of them met at the gate.

"Michael." Pete embraced his son warmly, then turned to Joanna. "I'd like you to meet Joanna Flemming. We were friends in high school."

Michael and Joanna shook hands while Joanna studied his handsome face. "You look a lot like your father when he was young," she said softly.

Pete introduced his son to Eve and Cliff, then said, "Well, why are we standing here in the cold when we should be getting ready for dinner?"

He led the way back to the house and the others followed, with Cliff bringing up the rear as he zigzagged around the cow pies that dotted the ground.

Pete, at the head of the table—with Joanna on his right and Betsy beside her—stood and the noisy chatter subsided as he cleared his throat and began to speak. "It's wonderful that our family can all be together for this holiday." His eyes rested briefly on Michael who sat next to Joanna. "And we're happy to have our friends share this meal. But most of all, this day we are thankful to have Robin with us and we owe our gratitude to you for that, Joanna." He laid his hand lightly on her shoulder and smiled at the little girl who sat in her father's lap. "So I'd like us all to join hands and bow our heads and offer our silent thanks to God for all our blessings."

Pete carved the turkey, surrounded by a platter of deviled eggs and dressing, and the plates were rotated to receive generous servings. Vegetables and rolls were passed while Rebecca and LaWanda served coffee and tea. Ursula and Ivana prepared plates for the little ones at the kitchen table.

"The turkey is delicious," Rebecca said and the others agreed while Joanna beamed proudly.

"And so nice and brown, but still moist," Ursula added. "What's your secret?"

"No secret," Joanna said, not meeting Betsy's eyes. "Just beginner's luck, I guess."

Pete's daughters refilled cups and glasses while the daughters-in-law brought servings of pie. Once again, the compliments were numerous and sincere.

"What delicious pie crust, Joanna," Rebecca commented as she took her first bite of pecan pie. "Almost as good as yours, Betsy."

"Oh, I'm not worried." Betsy lightly kicked Joanna under the table. "She has a way to go before she's any competition."

Suddenly realizing that LaWanda had not returned to the table, Joanna excused herself and went to look for her. She met her coming from the guest bedroom, looking frightened.

"LaWanda, what—"

"I think the baby, my water broke. I need..."

"Sit down, honey." She led her to the den sofa.

"I'll tell Bill to get your coat."

Joanna returned to the table and forced herself to speak calmly. "Bill, I left LaWanda in the den. She's not feeling well. I think it's time to take her to the hospital. Can you get her things?"

As Bill got up from the table, Pete also stood. "I'll drive you." He looked around at the others. "Please excuse me, and enjoy the rest of your dinner. Glad you could join us, Eve, Cliff, Betsy."

Pete, followed by Joanna, went to the den where Bill was assisting LaWanda into her coat. "We'll take the car, it's more comfortable than your van."

Bill nodded, and they started toward the garage but LaWanda stopped and turned toward Joanna. "Would you come, too?" she asked in a quivery voice.

"Of course, if you want me to," Joanna said quickly. She grabbed her coat and rushed back to offer a quick explanation to those still seated at the table before she left. Tears welled up in her eyes and threatened to spill over as she joined LaWanda at her request in the back seat of the car and put an arm protectively around her. This is what it meant to be a family. This was part of being a mother.

In record time they reached the hospital where LaWanda was quickly admitted. She was placed on a gurney and rolled toward the elevator, with Bill trotting along beside her. Joanna and Pete were ushered into the deserted waiting room.

He gave her a wry grin. "We've got to stop meeting like this."

She forced herself to smile back. "I'm just hoping for a happy outcome again."

Pete's brow furrowed. "It's too early for what's happened now."

"Was Robin early, too?" Joanna asked in a worried tone.

Pete shook his head. "No." Reading her unspoken concern, added, "this is no indication of another Down's Syndrome baby. LaWanda had German measles in the early stage of her last pregnancy."

Joanna nodded and reached for Pete's hand. "That must have been heartbreaking."

"Yes, at the time we were devastated. But Robin has been the joy of our family." Pete squeezed her hand. "And speaking of family, what a feast you prepared for our holiday dinner."

Joanna had the grace to blush but in the dim room Pete was unaware of it. "Well," she began slowly, "I have a confession to make."

"Perhaps you should be telling your sins to Michael. He's the priest in the family, you know," he teased.

For a moment, stark sadness overcame Joanna and she couldn't speak. Then she got a grip on her emotions and went on, "I had some help...from Betsy."

"I suspected as much," Pete patted her hand. "But it doesn't matter. Betsy's an old hand at putting together a meal to feed a houseful of children and you've had no call to do that till now."

"I never really learned to cook. The kitchen was my mother's domain."

He put his arm around her and pulled her close. "Your talent lies elsewhere. You do other things for children. You feed their minds and mold their lives. I've seen examples of your fine efforts, you know. You have no reason to be apologetic."

"Thank you," she said, feeling his words suffuse her with warmth.

He put a hand under her chin and lifted her face until she met his gaze. "Now, don't you feel better from having confessed?"

She smiled and nodded and he kissed her lightly and then continued.

"And while we're confessing, I want to add my

own thoughts. At dinner, I was observing that lawyer Eve brought today."

"Cliff Averill?"

"Yeah. I was thinking about how suited a man like him would be to you. He's well educated, a sharp dresser, socially adept, and has a prominent position. And from the looks he gave you from time to time, I think he is a damned sight more interested in you than Eve."

Joanna laughed, the musical sound reverberating in the quiet room. "Me? Don't be silly. I'm not his type at all."

"You're every man's type, my darling. You're perfect."

"Oh, Pete, be serious."

"I *am* serious. And for the life of me, I don't understand what you see in a Missouri dirt farmer. But even if I'm not as well-matched to you as the Cliff Averills in the world, no man could love you more than I do. And I'd never give you up to anyone without one hell of a fight."

Joanna put a gentle hand on his cheek. "You have nothing to fear. There's not a Cliff Averill in the world who can hold a candle to you in my mind."

She laid her head on his shoulder and he pulled her closer and whispered, "If this weren't a public place, I'd try to show you how right we are together."

"I'm already convinced," she assured him. "My heart has always known."

CHAPTER THIRTEEN

Joanna double-checked the items she had assembled on the dining table before packing them in a canvas tote bag. A large thermos of coffee, Styrofoam cups, ham sandwiches, chocolate bars, napkins and bottled water. Just as she zipped the bag, her doorbell rang.

Throwing open the door, she smiled. “Right on time. I was afraid the heavy traffic would slow you down.”

“Hello, my darling. Don’t you know nothing could make me late for a date with the woman I love?” He held a large white mum toward her. “For you.”

“Oh, Pete. How lovely. Will you pin it on, please?”

“Later.” He stepped inside and enfolded her in his arms, kissed her soundly, then expertly attached the flower to her coat. His hands lightly brushed her breast as he fastened the stem, sending a shiver of pleasure through her body. He held her away from him and his eyes traveled from her scarlet woolen cap and matching scarf to her heavy gray coat and black leather gloves and boots. “Wow. You look stunning.”

“Flattery will get you anything.” At his look of eager anticipation she hastily amended, “but not right now. We need to be going. There will be a mob at this first home game."

"As you wish, my love, but I'll hold you to that promise later." He moved to the table and picked up the canvas bag. "I'd say from the weight of this, you've packed enough to last a week instead of one evening."

She laughed. "The thermos is quite large but I thought we might need lots of coffee to keep warm."

He shook his head. "Coffee's good—" He gave her a seductive grin. "—but I've got my love to keep me warm."

Joanna grabbed the plaid blanket off the sofa and gave it to Pete. She locked her door and they hurried to Pete's car which he had left in front of the building.

He stashed the bag and blanket in back and got behind the wheel. Before he turned the ignition, he leaned toward Joanna and kissed her cheek. "I'm glad you asked me to come with you tonight. I haven't seen a live football game since my boys graduated college."

"Don't your grandkids play football?"

Pete shook his head. "Not yet. But with consolidation, there will be enough money in the school budget to add that to the curriculum."

Soon they joined the traffic that inched through the university gates and were directed to parking areas beyond. Pete and Joanna had a long walk across campus to the stadium. An abundance of autumn leaves still clung to the limbs of the towering oaks, their colors muted now. Bright orange, red, and yellow had segued into russet, burgundy, and gold. The wind rattled in the branches, releasing a blended potpourri that swirled and soared on a downward spiral.

"Oh, isn't this lovely?" Joanna gestured toward the falling fragments of color, her eyes sparkling with pleasure.

"You mean the leaves?" Pete asked softly. "I suppose so. I can't really appreciate nature's beauty when I have you to look at." He shifted the tote bag to the same arm that carried the blanket and took Joanna's hand.

As they drew closer to the stadium, the drum beats grew louder and they could hear the rising noise of the crowd. An aura of controlled excitement permeated the air.

By the time they waited in line and found their seats, the leaden gray clouds were spitting snow. Pete and Joanna snuggled together beneath the welcome warmth of the blanket as they watched the preliminary activity on the field.

"Do you attend many games?" Pete asked.

"Only a few each season. I really prefer basketball," Joanna told him, remembering the sight of Pete on Greenville's court and her on the sidelines cheering her heart out.

"Yeah, I'm partial to basketball myself." He grinned and she thought he must be remembering, too.

"But I guess I'll become a regular fan this season. I have a special interest in a student on the team."

"The guy I saw in your office that night?"

Joanna nodded. "Yes, Ted. He's our team's best player. He set a record for most touchdowns last year and pro football scouts are already making offers for him."

"Is he a senior now?"

"Yes, he was a transfer from a smaller college. Our coach recruited Ted his junior year. So if he can only keep his grades up and stay on the team this season, he should have his pick of the pros."

"What's the problem? Too much party time?"

"Oh, no. Ted's a good student but he has to hold down a job as well as a full load of classes. That doesn't leave much time to study."

"That's tough."

"And I've agreed to tutor him evenings in whatever subject he's getting low grades, which at the moment is History as well as English."

"Just what I'd expect you would do, Joanna. But doesn't that take most of your own free time?" Pete chided her.

"I can manage," she assured him. "Ted can't afford a paid tutor and I usually stay late at school anyway."

"It seems you always go beyond what's required. But that's just another reason I adore you." He removed his gloves and reached to squeeze her hand.

"Take mine off, too," she whispered. "I want to feel the warmth of your skin."

Their attention was caught by the announcer's shout of excitement as a Memphis State fullback received the ball and made a run for the goal. The player made it to the ten yard line before being brought down by Georgia Tech.

"What a play," the announcer was saying. "A long pass by Haverty and unbelievable catch by Sullivan who shot down the field like a low-flying jet till Robb and Jones stopped him at the ten yard line."

Joanna clenched her fists and stretched forward in an effort to see the player who lay on the bottom of the heap that kept growing as both teams converged on the white line.

"Oh, that looks brutal," she moaned.

Pete chuckled. "Is Sullivan your guy?"

"Yes, that's Ted." She took a deep breath, exhaled. "Well, *finally,* the referee is getting them off the poor kid."

"That's how the game is played, sweetheart. It's not a sport for sissies."

"Oh, look, Pete." She clutched his arm. "He isn't

getting up. Ted's hurt."

Pete patted her hand. "He'll be okay. Probably just got the breath knocked out of him."

A trainer and coach rushed the field and hovered over the prone body of Ted Sullivan. After what seemed to Joanna an agonizing length of time, Ted got up and with the two men on either side of him, limped off the field.

The ball was put back in play and the Tigers scored a touchdown on their second attempt. The game went on but Joanna's interest was focused on the bench where Ted sat with his head in his hands.

"He'll be fine," Pete assured her as they sat down again. "How about some coffee now to steady your nerves, huh?"

He uncapped the thermos and poured the steaming liquid and handed it to her.

"Thanks." Joanna gave him a tentative smile. "I guess it's a good thing I don't have a son." The minute the words left her lips, she drew a quick breath. "What I meant was—"

"Don't apologize for being a caring person." He grinned at her. "Mary Esther was a wreck every time our boys played any sport. It's the hovering mother syndrome, I guess."

They sipped their coffee in silence as the game went on. At halftime, with Memphis leading by fourteen points, they ate the sandwiches Joanna had packed and drank more coffee.

In the third quarter, Georgia Tech made their first touchdown. Then a kickoff to Memphis State was fumbled and the Bulldogs took the ball and managed to score again. Going into the final quarter the teams were tied. Both Tigers and Bulldogs fought fiercely for every inch they gained but neither scored again.

With only minutes left to play, Sullivan returned to the field, retrieved a long pass and ran toward the goal. The crowd went wild, shouting and screaming while the announcer kept up a running commentary on Sullivan's progress.

"Go, Ted, go! Go, Tiger, go!" The chant began and swelled to drown out all else. And go he did. Right over the goal line for the winning touchdown in the final seconds of the game.

Joanna gripped Pete's arm as they stood on the metal bleachers and shouted encouragement. And when Ted Sullivan crossed the line, Pete hugged her hard and planted a quick kiss on her cold lips.

"You're freezing," he said and scooped up the blanket and bag. "Let's get out of here."

"Not until I tell Ted how proud I am of him," Joanna said. "It shouldn't take long. He's still down on the field so if we hurry we can catch him before he goes to the locker room."

They made their way out of the stands onto the field, dodging the spectators who were mostly going the other way. Ted was surrounded by enthusiastic fans and it took a bit of maneuvering to get to the inner circle.

"You played a great game, Ted. I'm so proud of you," Joanna said and extended her hand.

The broad-shouldered jock, perspiration soaking his muddy uniform, turned his black-rimmed eyes toward the sound of her voice. Then he took a step and swept her up, whirled her around, and planted a kiss on her cheek.

"I owe you one, Doc. I wouldn't be here without you."

Joanna gave him a hearty hug. "Thank you, Ted. But you've worked hard. You earned the glory."

Pete thrust out his hand. "Good job, Ted. Congratulations."

Ted looked at the man beside Joanna and his eyes lit up with recognition. "Hey, the doc came through for me again, didn't she? Just like I'd hoped."

The crowd around the hero of the night clamored for his attention and Joanna and Pete moved on. With hands clasped to avoid separation, they joined the jostling crowd that surged toward the exit gate, resigned to a long trek back to the car.

After what seemed an eternity, Pete was able to maneuver onto the main street and head for Beekman Place. Traffic still moved at a snail's pace, as cars honked horns and people yelled from open windows in celebration.

He drove into a now-familiar overnight parking space and they collected the items from the back seat and went into the deserted lobby. As the elevator door closed and they began the ascent to fifth floor, Pete put his free arm around Joanna's waist and pulled her close.

"Have you ever made love in an elevator?" he whispered.

Joanna's eyes grew wide in surprise at the suggestion, then she laughed softly. "No, and I don't think this is the time or place to do so. I have to renew my lease soon."

He nodded solemnly. "Then I'll make an effort to restrain myself."

Inside the condo, he put down the bag and blanket and shrugged out of his jacket. Then he gently removed Joanna's coat and wrapped his arms around her.

"Hungry?" she asked.

"For you." He tilted her face and covered her mouth with his. The kiss was long and sensuous and she lost herself in the sensations it evoked. One of Pete's hands moved from her back to the lower edge of her bulky sweater and underneath to touch her skin. Slowly his gentle fingers found her breast and began an slow caress.

"Take it off," she whispered, her body straining

urgently for more of his touch on her skin.

Separating from her long enough to do her bidding, he raised the garment over her head and flung it carelessly toward the nearest chair. He stood for a moment, admiring the voluptuous mounds beneath the filmy lace of her bra, then peeled down the straps to reveal her bare breasts. He bent to kiss first one, then the other as she trembled with desire.

Then in a flurry of passion, they removed each other's clothes in frantic haste and Pete led her to the nearest loveseat, unmindful that its dimensions would scarcely accommodate his length.

"No." Joanna shook her head. "Here." And sank onto the plush white carpet and opened her arms to Pete in a gesture of welcome. He knelt beside her and laved her body with ardent kisses until she was mindless with wanting, then entered her and brought them to their peak of passion and beyond.

Panting from his exertion, Pete collapsed beside her and wrapped his arms around her. "I always think making love to you can't be any better but then you prove me wrong."

"That's because you're a wonderful lover, Pete. I feel so fortunate to have you in my life."

"We both are lucky to have found each other again. Just think, if you hadn't come to that last reunion we might never have known this happiness."

Joanna gave a slight shudder. "I don't even want to imagine that."

Pete held her closer. "Then don't. Because I'm here and I'm not going away. Well," he amended, "at least not tonight and then only as far as Greenville."

"I'm glad." She stroked his face, feeling the faint stubble on his cheek. "Are you hungry now?"

He chuckled. "Is that a trick question? I have satisfied the craving I had for you with this appetizer but I still have a desire for more. Still, I think an omelet would taste good right now. And then we'll crawl into that lovely four-poster in the bedroom and continue on to the main course."

"How about hash browns with that? The omelet, I mean, not the main course."

"Sure." He stood and pulled Joanna up beside him and gave her a tender kiss, then a pat on her shapely bottom. "Why don't we get our clothes on, just in case of visitors—" Joanna winced at the reminder. "—and I'll help you prepare the ingredients for the omelet?"

"I think I'll just get a robe," Joanna said, "and hang these things up." She glanced at the clothes lying on the floor in tangles and gave Pete a wry smile.

Joanna took bell peppers, onions, and mushrooms from the refrigerator. In anticipation of feeding Pete, she had shopped for more groceries than she usually kept on hand. A bag of frozen hash-browns went into a skillet while Pete chopped ingredients to add to the eggs she prepared.

"Wheat toast or rye?" she asked as she filled the coffee maker and plugged it in.

"The usual," he said as he closed the lid on the omelet pan.

Joanna nodded and assembled the bread and buttered it for toasting. They had fallen into a pattern of comfortable familiarity much like a marriage relationship, she imagined.

Except for making love, which still surprised her with its intensity.

Discussing the highlights of the football game, they completed the impromptu meal. While Joanna rinsed and Pete loaded the dishwasher, he suddenly broke the comfortable silence. "Have you ever considered living anywhere else, Joanna?"

At her puzzled look, he went on. "I don't mean this condo, I meant another town. Perhaps teaching at another college."

She thought for a long moment before answering. "No, I really haven't." She didn't know where this was leading and she was afraid to ask why he wanted to know.

Pete let the subject drop and they took second cups of coffee into the living room and watched the last half of a TV sitcom. When the commercials began at the half hour, Pete hit the mute button and yawned.

"Sleepy?" Joanna asked in a teasing tone.

"Not on your life, lady. Why would I want to sleep when I am going to bed with a beautiful woman I can make love to?"

"Beats me." She snuggled against him on the loveseat and lifted her face, her mouth inviting his kiss.

He bent to touch her lips with his tongue, then moved to her jaw and left a trail of fire to her earlobe. She wrapped her arms around his neck and his hand found the opening in her velour robe and began a slow circle of her breast.

Her breath caught in a low moan at the sensation of his touch. "Pete, what you do to me. How can I want you so much?"

"Because I want *you* so much it makes me crazy," he said and pulled her closer. "Let's go to bed."

"The floor is closer," she whispered.

"Been there, done that." He stood and pulled her to him. "This time I'm going to make love to you at leisure, not grope you like a sex-starved stud."

"Whatever you say," she purred, "but if we're going to make a night of it, I'd like to suggest a warm shower first."

"Great idea. And followed by a soothing oil massage."

"With scented candles burning. And soft music."

He took her hand. "Lady, you have set the scene for a night of seduction. Let's start the performance."

Together, they headed toward the bedroom leaving the soundless TV images flickering in the darkened room beyond.

In the early hours of morning Joanna lay awake in Pete's arms, listening to his steady breathing that kept time with the second hand on the bedside clock. Being with Pete fulfilled the dreams and hopes she had long ago abandoned. He was all she had ever wanted and more. But could they go on this way without taking their relationship to another level? Would Pete be willing to do that when he realized that this was all she had to give? Tonight he had asked a question that made her think he might be hoping for more. And if she said no, then what would happen to them?

Pete stirred, and she snuggled closer in his arms. She thought of the insurmountable thing that lay between them. The thing she could never reveal to him that would drive him away from her forever. Silent tears spilled down her cheeks in the semi-darkness. She would savor every moment with him against the time that must inevitably come.

They slept late and woke to make love, then shower together, and finally made their way to the kitchen for coffee.

Joanna prepared fresh fruit and set the table while Pete made pancakes.

"These peaches won't taste farm fresh but it was the best I could do here in the city," she told him.

"Well, city girl, we don't have fresh peaches on the farm in November either."

"Okay, farm boy, I admit I didn't think of that or I wouldn't have apologized."

"I could get accustomed to these sleepover weekends." Pete grinned at her as he slid another pancake onto the platter and poured a pool of thin batter into the skillet.

Slathering on a generous pat of real butter, Joanna nodded.

"Me, too."

"But when spring comes, it won't be easy to get away from the farm. Not even for one night."

"But I have time off between spring and summer semesters, and again in early autumn," she said as she smiled at him.

"I'd like it to be more, Joanna. Being with you is addictive. I never seem to get enough."

"You know the saying, Pete, familiarity breeds contempt," she told him lightly.

"Not for me it wouldn't," he countered with conviction. "The more time I have with you, the more I want."

She was saved from further discussion as Pete placed the last pancake on the platter and they sat down to eat before the food got cold. This time she was certain where Pete's thoughts were leading. No matter how much she wished it so, things would not stay the same forever.

CHAPTER FOURTEEN

It seemed to Joanna that the season's first holiday segued into the other two with almost no space between. She was still basking in Pete's lavish praise for the successful Thanksgiving meal she had managed with Betsy's surreptitious help when she realized another family dinner loomed just ahead. Fortunately, Pete announced that in appreciation for all her efforts, his family had insisted on having a Christmas buffet with everyone bringing food. Now she was looking forward to the remaining holidays with much more enthusiasm.

Eve set cups of steaming spearmint leaf tea on the snack bar and took her place on a rattan stool opposite Joanna. "How long do you plan to be away?"

"Until after New Year's." Joanna took a tentative taste. "Mmmm, it's as good as it smells. I hope my plants won't be a bother for that long?"

"No problem. I'm not going anywhere, except out to dinner on Christmas Eve. Cliff is finally taking me to meet his daughter. Did I tell you she's adopted?" Joanna shook her head. "Cliff says he's waited so long to introduce me because the girl is obsessed with finding her birth mother and he doesn't approve of what she's doing, but I suspect he's worried that she won't approve of me."

"Why not?"

Eve smiled grimly. "She'll probably think I'm

after his money."

"Well, are you?" Joanna teased. "With that Mercedes and those custom-tailored suits, I'd say he's got plenty of it."

"Yeah, and that bothers me." She sighed dramatically. "But our signs are compatible and Marvella is getting good vibes about this relationship."

"But are you getting good vibes?" Joanna asked skeptically.

"Am I! He's terrific in bed. Whoever said older men—"

"I didn't mean just sex..." Joanna waved her hand to stop the flow of words she wasn't sure she wanted to hear.

"Well, it is true we disagree about almost everything but we're working on that. In fact, Cliff is attending a Save The Planet rally with me next weekend. We've finally found *two* things we agree on." She sipped her tea. "But enough about my love life. Would you like me to look in on your mother while you are away?"

"That would be very nice, if you're sure it won't be too inconvenient."

"I'll be glad to do it, Joanna. So forget school and your other responsibilities and just enjoy the holidays."

"Thanks, Eve." Joanna finished her tea and stood up. "I really should get started. The weatherman promised snow and I don't want to get caught in a snowstorm."

The two women wished each other a Merry Christmas and said goodbye. Then Joanna hastily gathered her bags and boxes of gifts and loaded the car.

Traffic was heavy as she approached downtown, crossed the bridge into the edge of West Memphis, and headed north. Joanna switched on the radio and hummed along with the familiar carols, feeling happier than she could remember being since the Christmas of her senior year in high school.

Snow began falling—huge soft flakes that drifted lazily from the dark sky—and she turned on the windshield wipers. Soon the fields were white; bushes along the road took on grotesque shapes and the wind blew drifts against the fence rows. Car lights came out of the swirling whiteness, crept past her; then silence returned except for the radio that crackled with static now. Impatiently, she switched it off, giving her full attention to the road.

The sound of icy needles hitting the hood of the car alerted her to the change from snow to sleet. Where was she? The signs along the Interstate were blotted out by poor visibility and she could only estimate from straining to see the hands of her watch that she had about half an hour yet to go. Suddenly remembering that she had failed to take into account her slower speed because of the storm, she revised her projection to nearer an hour.

Joanna tapped her brakes and went into a minor skid, proving her suspicion that the road's surface was coated with ice. Nothing passed her for miles except a semi, spraying muddy slush against the driver's window and further decreasing her ability to see. Still the sleet kept falling, blowing against the windshield with a vengeance. She'd wanted a white Christmas, but not just yet.

She debated calling Pete on her cell phone which lay on the seat beside her but she needed to keep her eyes on the road and both hands on the wheel. And it would only cause him worry to know how bad the road conditions were.

After what seemed like hours instead of less than one, Joanna recognized a large partially obscured sign indicating the Greenville exit just ahead. She was already driving slowly enough to turn which was just as well since braking would be impossible. Leveling out of the off-ramp curve, Joanna breathed a sigh of relief at the sight of a snowplow coming toward her on the two-lane highway. Thank heavens the road crew had already cleared the highway into town. She would worry about the road to Pete's house when she got to it.

At the corner of Yokely's Drugs, a black truck like Pete's sat next to the curb. It pulled out behind her, horn honking, and flashed its lights. It was Pete! He passed her and kept going, slowly so that she could keep him in sight, his truck tires making tracks that she could follow to the farm.

Turning into the cleared driveway, Joanna parked the car inside the open garage and shut off the ignition, feeling weak from fatigue and tension. Before she could move, Pete was opening the car door, reaching for her, and enveloping her in a warm embrace.

"I was so worried about you," he said softly. "I called Eve and found out what time you left Memphis. And I tried your cell phone number several times but there's a dead airspace for miles between Greenville and the river. If you hadn't arrived soon I was ready to call the Highway Patrol to put out an APB for you." He covered her face with kisses, then took her hand. "Come on inside, I'll get your things later."

In the den, a fire blazed in the fireplace, its mantel festooned with live greenery. Pete shrugged off his coat, then removed Joanna's, pausing to admire her cranberry cashmere sweater and white tapered slacks.

"God, you look wonderful."

"So do you." She touched the textured navy sweater he wore and he reached for her hand and pulled her to him, covering her mouth with his for a deep passionate kiss. She wrapped her arms around his neck and pressed closer, her body aching for his caresses. Together they knelt in front of the fireplace, each slowly undressing the other, kindling a flame that warmed them more than the heat from the blazing fire.

Afterward, Pete wrapped her in an afghan from the sofa and went to get hot cocoa and sandwiches which they ate as they watched the burning logs and listened to Christmas carols. Outside the wind howled and the sleet became snow again and continued falling.

"I meant to feed you first," he said with a wry grin.

Joanna laughed softly. "I think you had your priorities in order."

"We have a long afternoon and evening ahead of us before the family shows up," Pete told her. "Perhaps we can continue where we left off before lunch."

Joanna pretended to study his proposition before she answered. "An interesting idea, but first I want to get my things from the car. I've brought an Amalgamation Cake and I don't want it to freeze."

Pete beamed at her. "We haven't had one of those since Mary—How did you...?"

"Betsy gave me the recipe," Joanna answered. There was no need to tell him that she had gotten so engrossed in adding all those spices, nuts, raisins, coconut, and jam that she had forgotten to include flour and her first attempt had turned into baked rubber. Practice made perfect and the second one was a cake to be proud of.

"It's Michael's favorite."

"Betsy told me. When do you expect him?"

"Not until tomorrow; he's saying Mass tonight. But then, LaWanda and Bill will be absent, too, though Robin is at Rebecca's so she'll be in the middle of it all."

"Nothing yet on when the baby will be here?"

Pete shook his head. "The doctor wanted to wait as long as possible, give it a chance to come naturally, but if it doesn't happen soon—" He shrugged. "—they'll have to take it."

"I'm sure it's been difficult for her to stay in bed these last weeks," Joanna said, "especially the waiting to see if the baby will be okay."

"The heartbeat is strong; that's all we know."

"Everything will be all right." Joanna brushed back a lock of Pete's hair and he reached for her hand and kissed it, then helped her up, and they dressed and went to unload Joanna's car.

Pete and Joanna deposited their armloads of gaily wrapped packages under the tall pine that stood at one end of the long living room, laden with bells and bows that reflected its twinkling lights. "Oh, Pete, it's magnificent. It almost touches the ceiling."

"Cut it right here on the farm." Pete stepped back to admire it with her. "First tree we've had since, well, Rebecca's done Christmas the last few years. But this year is special." He put an arm around her. "So Betsy helped me decorate it before she left."

"Left?"

"She and Lana are spending the holidays in St. Louis with the twins. Decided at the last minute. Said she just couldn't handle it at home this first year since Walt..." He left the words unsaid and bent to move a package that was in danger of toppling over.

"Pete?" Joanna asked solemnly, and he stood and looked at her. "Will your children mind that I'm here for Christmas?"

"Of course not. They like you, Joanna, surely you can sense that, can't you?"

"Well, just the same, Christmas is such a special

time for families to be together."

Pete pulled her closer. "You have a place in my heart, same as they, Joanna. Only you were there first." He tilted her chin, kissed her lightly, and whispered, "Have I ever made love to you under a Christmas tree?"

"I don't think so." Joanna laughed softly. "But I have a feeling you'll correct that oversight now."

With exquisite tenderness he took her face in his hands, kissed her closed eyelids, whispered love words in her ear as his hands caressed her, pleasuring every secret place. The lights glistened from the fragrant pine, illuminating their entwined bodies as carols softly played in counterpoint to the ancient music of lovers.

Later that evening, Pete prepared steaks on an indoor grill and they ate again in front of the fire. When they had sated themselves with food and loaded the dishwasher, Joanna's drooping eyelids betrayed her fatigue.

"Let's go to bed, my love. Tomorrow will be a madhouse around here and I can see that you need sleep."

"I am exhausted," Joanna admitted. "It is always this way when classes end for the holidays."

He took her hand and led her into the hallway and hesitated. "Do you want to sleep in..." His voice trailed off as he gestured toward the master suite.

She looked beyond the door to the king-size bed and shook her head. "The other room is fine." She felt more at ease in the guest room and surely tomorrow when his children came it would be better if her things were there. She gave him a wicked grin. "This way, I can be sure you'll sleep close all night long."

"Be warned, you may not get much sleep."

"I won't complain."

When they had undressed, Pete tucked her in

and crawled in beside her, fitting his body to her, spoon fashion. "Goodnight, Joanna. You know I want you every time I touch you, but I'm only going to hold you tonight. We have plenty of time for loving when you are rested."

Joanna murmured in agreement, her eyelids already closing as she snuggled against his warm body and fell asleep.

CHAPTER FIFTEEN

Pete's children brought food for the dinner and to further expedite the feeding of so many and get on with opening gifts, the meal was served buffet-style. Dishes for the main course were placed on the dining table, which was draped in a red cloth and decorated with matching candles and pine bows. Joanna's Amalgamation Cake claimed the place of honor in the center of the kitchen table, surrounded by assorted pies, cookies, fruit salad, and eggnog.

Some of the adults were seated at card tables, others used TV trays, and the children sat on the long hearth or cross-legged on the carpet. It seemed to Joanna as if people were everywhere as she happily watched and listened to Pete's family, while she held Robin in her lap, feeding her from their shared plate.

When the phone rang, Kyle answered, then called to Pete from the kitchen. "For you, Dad."

Pete talked for a few minutes, holding one hand over his ear exposed to the noise, then came back into the den. "That was Michael," he said to those close enough to hear. "He won't make it tomorrow. Interstate's closed up that way."

Joanna made a sound of sympathy and Pete patted her hand. "I told him that you made his favorite cake, and he said be sure to freeze a large piece of it for him."

Joanna smiled. "Consider it done."

Before they finished dessert, there was another call for Pete and this time his brows were drawn together in a frown when he returned. "What is it?" Joanna asked quickly.

"That was Bill. He's taking LaWanda to the hospital. Her pains started, and they're twenty minutes apart."

"Will you need to go?"

Pete shook his head. "No, they can get to Cape faster if they don't have to wait for me. They've got chains on the van and the road's open so they should make it fine." He took a deep breath, raised his voice. "Okay, everyone. Let's adjourn to the living room and see what Santa left in all those packages under the tree."

The children squealed with excitement and made hasty work of disposing of their colorful paper plates and cups. Pete grabbed a fur-trimmed red hat and lifted Robin in his arms. "Jolly, ho, ho, ho. And away we go."

Robin entwined her chubby arms around Pete's neck and laughed. "Go, Gwampie, go."

Pete reached to pull Joanna to her feet. "Come on, Joanna. I need two helpers to pass out gifts. Robin tends to want to open all of them herself."

The grownups followed the eager children, and when all were gathered around the tree, they sang "Silent Night" and then Pete and his helpers dispensed the gifts. Soon a mountain of crumpled paper and ribbons lay all around and Joanna wondered how everyone could ever keep their gifts separated from the others, but they appeared to have no trouble doing so.

The children played with a minimum of confusion but at a maximum noise level, or so it seemed to Joanna who was unused to so much frenetic activity. The men returned to the den for more eggnog while the women packed the remaining food and put the kitchen to order.

"Wonderful cake, Joanna," Ivana told her as she snatched another bite from the plate before Joanna put a cover on it. "I haven't tasted one of those since Richard's mom..." She let the words die and a small strained silence followed.

"I really should have made one myself before now for Dad and Michael," Rebecca said and smiled at Joanna, "but the recipe is so much bother I just kept making excuses. Thanks for taking on the job."

"It was my pleasure," Joanna answered, and added silently, *what you don't know about my first disastrous attempt won't hurt either of us.*

When the phone rang again, the women looked at each other expectantly.

"Maybe the baby—" Rebecca began just as Pete appeared in the doorway.

"It's for you, Joanna. You can take it in the bedroom."

She put down the dishcloth she was holding and quickly made her way to the phone. *Surely not my mother....?* "Hello?"

"Miss Flemming? This is Grace Beasley, at Oakwood Manor?"

It is my mother. They wouldn't call on Christmas Eve unless..."Yes, Mrs. Beasley. What is it?"

"Well, I wouldn't bother you but there was a man and woman here a while ago and, uh, the woman said she was a friend of yours?"

"Yes, that would be Eve Whitfield. She said she was going to see Mother today."

"She brought some things for Mrs. Flemming and she spent quite a while with her."

That would be like Eve to try and bring a little cheer to an invalid. "So, that's all? You were just wanting to make certain about the visitors?"

"Yes, but well, the man who was with her?"

Cliff Averill, no doubt. "Yes, Eve's friend. A very nice gentleman."

"He, uh, asked a lot of questions about Mrs. Flemming. Like what was her maiden name and where she was from. He said he thought she might be kin to his elderly aunt and I told him what he wanted to know. But after they left, you know, I got to thinking it seemed kinda strange and maybe I shouldn't have without asking you."

After a brief silence while she tried to absorb the information, Joanna said with as much assurance as she could muster, "I'm sure it's all right, Mrs. Beasley, but I appreciate you calling to tell me. Merry Christmas."

Still holding the phone, a feeling of apprehension swept over Joanna. Why would Cliff Averill ask the nurse about her mother? Why hadn't he simply asked her what he wanted to know? She supposed it was the district attorney training in him to be surreptitious instead of forthright. But she would definitely mention this to Eve when she got back to Memphis.

"Is everything okay?" Pete waited for her at the door to the den, his brow knitted in a worried frown.

She smiled to reassure him. "It was the nursing home. They wanted to check with me about my mother's visitors."

"That would be—" He began and they finished together. "Eve and Cliff."

Urging and cajoling, the parents finally managed to get their children into coats and scarves and mittens and they all piled into cars and vans and headed for Greenville for midnight Mass.

Pete's truck brought up the rear of the procession, with Joanna beside him holding Robin. Snow was still falling and the drifts obscured the edges of the road, but Lee and Rebecca led the way in their four-wheel drive and the others followed in their tracks.

The town was festively alight with tinseled poles and multi-colored bulbs blinking from darkened storefronts. Ahead, the stained glass windows of St. Joseph's cast pastel images on the pristine snow and from the bell tower chimes rang out in the stillness.

The church was packed to capacity on this holy night and Joanna and Pete wedged into a pew with the rest of the family just as Father Saffer intoned his welcome. The crowd grew silent and the priest began the service with Pete and his family repeating the words, kneeling and standing in practiced unison. Then the notes of the organ heralded the pure high voices of the choir whose lighted candles swayed in measured movement as they traveled from the sacristy the length of the sanctuary and mounted steps to the loft. Joanna thought she had never heard music so beautiful. She was filled with an overwhelming love for God that she had never experienced in all the sermons she had endured by her father's command.

Outside St. Joseph's Pete and Joanna said their goodbyes to his family as she surrendered a sleeping Robin to Rebecca's arms. Driving back to the farm in the deep groves now partially covered with new snow, Pete reached for Joanna's hand in the darkness, and they rode in silence, lost in the wonder of this night and the miracle that had brought them back together.

Pete parked the truck beside the garage and opened Joanna's door. "Oh, Pete," she said softly, "isn't it beautiful?" She held her hands up, palms open to catch a handful of feathery flakes. "Could we walk for a bit?"

Wordlessly, he took Joanna's hand and guided her through the trees in a wide path around the house. They traveled through drifts that reached almost to their knees and she scooped up a handful of wet snow to taste; then impulsively lay down on the blanket of white and moved her arms slowly to make shadowed imprints at either side. "Come on, make a snow angel," she coaxed.

"I'll be happy to accept your invitation," Pete answered but instead of following her example, he dropped to his knees above her and kissed the snowflakes from her face. "I have never made love to you in a snowstorm, have I?" he mumbled huskily against her ear.

Her laughter was an echo of St. Joseph's bells. "No, but I'd like you to."

Pete shrugged off his coat and placed it beneath her, then slipped her slacks and bikinis below her hips.

"Take them off," she demanded.

"You'll freeze," he warned.

"No," she gasped, wanting him inside her, urging him to fulfill her consuming need.

Their bodies joined in fervent heat as unmindful of the cold, they rode their passion to ecstatic heights unreached before, then lay shivering in each other's arms. "How can it be better every time?" Pete asked in awe. "It was enough just to find you again, but this..." He left the sentence unfinished and pulled her to her feet, wrapped his coat around her. "Let's go inside, my love, and drink a toast and see what's left under the tree."

By mutual agreement, they'd chosen to wait and open their gifts for each other after the family had gone. Sitting before the fire, sipping eggnog generously laced with whiskey, Joanna smiled as Pete placed a white stocking in her hands and bent to kiss her.

"Merry Christmas, Joanna. I love you."

"And I love you," she whispered and reached to touch his cheek still flushed from the cold and their heat.

The stocking contained a beautiful pair of black leather gloves and a gold case for business cards engraved with her name. “Thank you, Pete, it’s just what—”

“There’s something else. Reach deeper.”

Joanna’s fingers closed over a small box in the toe and slowly pulled it out. Even before she opened the lid she knew the ring would be a solitaire but she was aghast at the size and brilliance of it and the intricate design of the rubies that bordered it. “Oh, Pete.”

He took the ring from her, slipped it on the third finger of her left hand. “I want this to signify my love and commitment to you, Joanna. I want you to be my wife but whether your answer is yes or no, please wear the ring as long as we’re together.”

Joanna’s heart hammered so loudly in her ears she could scarcely hear her own voice answer. “Pete, I never expected, I wish with all my heart I could say yes, but...I think the only answer at this stage in our lives is to go on the way we are.”

Pete bowed his head and the silence between them was deafening. Finally he spoke. “It will be your choice.”

The phone shattered the emotional tension with insistent shrillness and Pete rose with evident relief to answer it. In a moment he came back and stood before Joanna, willing her to look at him.

“That was Bill. My new grandson was born while we were at Mass. And Peter James Acree and his mother are doing fine.” He gave her a lopsided grin. “At least one of my prayers was answered tonight.” He held out a hand to her and she stood and took it. “It’s Christmas morning, Joanna. Come on to bed.”

Lying in the darkness encircled by Pete’s arms, Joanna blinked back stinging tears. The unfamiliar diamond felt as heavy on her finger as the stone that weighed heavy in her heart. What irony that the thing that bound them together would forever keep them apart. Belatedly she remembered her own gifts to Pete, still lying unopened beneath the lighted tree. Perhaps it didn't matter because the gift he wanted was not hers to give.

CHAPTER SIXTEEN

"This isn't what I had planned for us to do while you were in Memphis, Bets." Joanna indicated the Spartan hospital room where she lay propped against pillows, her white afghan draping her shoulders, an open book lying beside her.

"Don't apologize. I'm just glad I was already here to be with you." Betsy sat in a leather chair close beside the bed.

"I'm glad, too. If you hadn't insisted I get the spotting checked, I would have assumed it was early menopause symptoms and ignored it."

"Never ignore abnormal bleeding." Betsy smiled. "But as your doctor told you, it may be just an ovarian cyst which can be easily removed."

"He also said it could be cancer," Joanna grimaced. "I'm scared, Bets."

Betsy reached to pat her hand. "Of course you are but the risk of that is very small."

"But if it should be..." She let her voice trail off.

"There's always chemo and radiation." Betsy shook her head. "Just listen to us, letting our imaginations run wild. Let's not borrow trouble."

"I keep thinking of Pete. He's been through this already with Mary Esther."

"Yes, and that experience has prepared him to be very supportive now. And speaking of Pete, when is he coming?"

Joanna glanced toward the window at the falling snowflakes that had created white silhouettes against the dark background of the building. "He should be here soon, unless the storm has delayed him."

"Miss Flemming?" A nurse stood in the doorway, a chart in her hand. "I need to ask you a few questions."

Betsy stood and squeezed Joanna's hand. "I'll be going now. Eve will be expecting me soon. Wish you were having dinner with us."

Joanna smiled. "Me, too. Have fun."

The nurse took the vacated chair and clicked her pen. She confirmed the information printed on the form which Joanna had already completed, then added, "Just a few more questions and we'll be finished.

"Is there any history of heart problems in your family?"

"No. Well, my father died of a stroke."

"Cancer?"

"No."

"Diabetes?"

"None."

"And have you ever had surgery before?"

Joanna shook her head.

"Do you have children?"

The verbal question took Joanna by surprise even though she had answered it falsely many times before on various forms. But this was different; she was about to undergo surgery related to her reproductive system. It seemed important that she tell the truth. She hesitated, stared at the pen poised above the chart, before she answered. "Yes, one child."

"Age?"

Another pause although the answer was on her tongue immediately. "Thirty."

"Sex?"

It seemed strange to be saying the word aloud. "Female."

"Natural or cesarean birth?"

"Natural."

"And your present marital status?"

The word came quickly without premeditation. "Single."

"There, we're all done. I'll just let you get back to your reading now. You'll get a light supper, then no fluids after midnight. Your surgeon, Dr. Jacobs?" The nurse looked to Joanna for verification and she nodded "—will be in to talk with you later, and so will the anesthesiologist."

"Thank you." Joanna watched the crisp white uniform disappear from view with a quiet swishing of rubber-soled shoes on the shiny tile.

A moment of panic seized her and she suddenly wanted to call the woman back and deny what she had just said. Never in all these thirty years had she told a living soul what she had revealed to this stranger. Only her mother and father had ever known that she had given birth to Peter Damron's baby.

A painful sob tore at her throat, struggling for release but she managed to silence it. She had long ago cried until all her tears were gone but admitting aloud just now that she had a daughter made the reality of it hit her like a sledge hammer. Somewhere a thirty year old she called Jennifer Bernadette existed that she would never know. Never be able to wrap her arms around. Never be able to tell how much she was loved.

Tears streamed down her face and she angrily swiped at them. She'd longed to look for her—until she found Pete again. After she'd seen him with his other children, seen the love he had for them, she had known he could never understand her giving their baby away. And though she loved him with all of her soul, she would never marry him with that guilty secret between them.

Now she was facing an uncertain future and she was glad she'd saved the letter the adoption agency had asked her to write in case her baby ever found her. Some girls had left their letters with the agency but she had kept hers. And for several years she had added a savings bond to the envelope on birthdays in hopes one day she could give it to her daughter. Until then, it remained in safekeeping with her attorney.

With determination, she forced herself to stop dwelling on the past that might have been and focus on the present that was enough to cope with for now. Since she was admitted this afternoon, she'd had her vital signs checked, been weighed, visited by a chaplain, and interviewed. It was just as well she had insisted Betsy have dinner with Eve since there would have been no time to talk anyway. She looked at the dark sky outside the large window, then at her watch. Only four and it was almost dark. She wondered what was keeping Pete. He should have been here by now.

With a sigh, she opened the book and resumed reading just as a white-coated orderly entered, consulted a chart on the tray he carried, and asked, "Joanna?"

"Yes?"

"I'm here to take a little blood." He removed one of the pillows from behind her. "Would you lie down, please?"

Joanna looked from the large hypodermic syringe he held to the tray of empty vials he had set on the bedside table. "Are you going to fill all those?"

Ignoring her question, he continued smoothly, "Now just lie back and stretch that arm out, and make a nice fist while I swab this spot with a little alcohol, that's the way...there, that didn't hurt too much, did it?"

Joanna flinched, gritted her teeth as the sting of the needle in the bend of her elbow sent a sharp pain up her arm. With fascination, she saw the dark red fluid slowly fill the vial. Then the orderly switched to another and repeated the procedure until there were none empty.

"There now, that's a good girl, Joanna." He removed the needle with a flourish, swabbed the puncture wound again, and slapped a bandage over it. "Thank you."

"You're welcome," Joanna responded to his retreating back with what she supposed was the proper hospital etiquette, then wondered why on earth she felt it necessary to be polite to someone who had pierced her with a needle and drained half her life's blood. It suddenly dawned on her that she would be losing a lot more blood than those ominous-looking vials had contained. She shuddered; it was not a happy thought.

"Joanna." Pete stole softly into the room, stood looking fondly at the woman lying in the narrow bed.

Her eyes flew open at the sound of his voice. "Pete, I was beginning to worry about you."

He set down the large shopping bag he carried, then pulling off his coat, tossed it on the nearest chair and bent to kiss her. "There was a wreck on the interstate. Had traffic blocked for miles, but I finally got around it."

"Ooooh, you're cold." With her own warm fingers, she reached to cover his hands that held her face.

"It's snowing hard out there." He nodded toward the window. "Temp's dropped ten degrees since I left Greenville. They've forecast a real winter storm."

"Just what we need, to get snowbound in the hospital," she said with a wry smile.

"As long as we're together." He kissed her again, then reached for the bag as he said, "I've brought you something. Robin sent it." He pulled out the honey-colored bear Joanna had chosen when she and Pete had been in Branson and placed it in Joanna's arms. "A loan until you're well again."

"How sweet." She buried her face in the animal's soft neck, brushing her tears against its fur.

Pete bent to hug her against his chest and reached into the bag again. "And here's something that you don't have to return."

He gave Joanna a square box and she carefully removed its wrappings, lifted the lid, and gasped at the exquisite piece of workmanship as she lifted out the delicate music box. It was a miniature porcelain carousel studded with tiny rubies that caught the waning light like points of fire.

"It's beautiful."

He reached to take the carousel from her and wind it up, then set it on the table beside her. A haunting melody played as the tiny horses began to revolve around the center pole. As she watched, entranced, Joanna remembered Eve's words and whispered, "We only go around once." She looked at Pete, eyes brimming with happy tears. "I love you, Pete."

Pete wrapped her in a fierce embrace, covering her face with warm kisses, then their lips met and the kiss deepened to a passionate message written in tongues. Suddenly, Pete disengaged himself from her and shook his head. "We'd better stop this before I crawl into bed with you and shock the medical profession." He pulled the recliner chair closer to the bed. "Has Bets been gone long?"

"Not long. Eve's making dinner for her, then she's spending the night there so you can sleep at my place."

"Joanna." Pete took her hand, stroked it gently.

"I want to stay with you every minute until they come for you in the morning."

"But Pete—" Joanna began a feeble protest but he laid a finger against her lips.

"I came to take care of you so you won't need to be afraid."

"How did you know...?" Joanna whispered.

"Because we all fear the unknown," Pete answered. "But I'm here with you and everything will be all right."

Joanna took his hand, held it against her cheek. It was warm and firm; she could feel the steady rhythm of his heart beating even in this furthermost part of him and she was comforted.

Pete met her trusting gaze with calm assurance. "Everything will be all right, Joanna. Nothing bad is going to happen to the woman I loved and lost and have found again."

With Pete beside her, his presence like a sentinel guarding her from fear, Joanna slept soundly through the night. She awoke to the unfamiliar sounds of the hospital just as the first light of day streamed through the open blinds. Pete, in the recliner chair next to her bed, still slept, his hand lying loosely on her arm.

She could hear the traffic noise of the city seven floors below and in the distance, a siren wailed and gradually grew louder. Her throat felt dry and she swallowed, wishing for a drink of water.

"Good morning." A different nurse glided in on silent feet, popped a thermometer into her mouth before she could reply and lifted her wrist to check her pulse. Startled, Pete withdrew his hand and sat up. Taking in his surroundings and orienting himself, he looked at Joanna and smiled. "Sleep well?"

"Bet—"

"Keep your mouth closed, dear."

Joanna looked at Pete and nodded, then gave her attention to the nurse who was speaking again. "Someone will be coming to prep you for surgery very soon. Then you'll get a sedative to help you relax before you go down." She slipped the thermometer from Joanna's lips, recorded her temperature, and left the room.

Pete passed a hand over the stubble on his face as he rose. "I'm going to step into the bathroom and get presentable, and go down to the snack shop while you're busy, then I'll be back." He bent to kiss her and she welcomed his moist lips on hers.

As Pete reached the door, he almost collided with Betsy. "Am I too late to see Joanna?" she asked without any preliminary greeting.

"No, they're getting her ready for surgery."

"Thank God. I was afraid I'd missed seeing her." She shook her head. "The snow has traffic slowed to a crawl."

"Care for a cup of coffee?"

"Later. Right now I'm going to sit with Joanna." At Pete's skeptical look, she added, "It's just girl stuff. They won't mind if I stay."

Joanna smiled as Betsy came into the room. "Aren't you out terribly early, Bets?"

"I'm a farm girl, remember? But after I saw what morning rush hour is like, I decided Pete was smart to spend the night here."

"Did you and Eve have a fun evening?"

"Yeah, but we missed you being with us. Eve said she'd be over before you get out of surgery, and to tell you Marvella says it will go well."

Joanna nodded, grateful for the psychic's prediction.

The nurse came back to begin the pre-op procedures."We'll be getting ready to go downstairs in a few minutes," she said, "so I'd like you to roll over and I'll just give you a quick jab in your hip.

There, all finished. That wasn't too bad, was it?"

Betsy squeezed Joanna's hand. "I'm going down for a cup of coffee. I'm sure Pete will be back in a few minutes. Hang in there, Joanna. I'll see you when you get back from the party."

"Some party," Joanna answered groggily as the unaccustomed sedative began to take effect.

Betsy and Pete met again in the doorway to Joanna's room.

"You look worse than the patient," Betsy observed in an undertone. "Life is rough, isn't it?"

Pete nodded. "I'd like to write the script for a while. I don't like the job somebody up there is doing right now."

"It'll get better," Betsy assured him as he walked toward Joanna's bed and she continued on toward the elevator.

"I'm back now." It was Pete's voice that spoke but the face that hovered above her was blurred beyond recognition. Then he bent to kiss her and his mouth, warm and possessive, left no doubt that it was her beloved. "I love you, Joanna," he whispered against her ear. "You're going to be fine. And I'll be waiting for you right here so hurry back."

She tried to reach for his hand but her arm felt heavy and she couldn't even lift her fingers. Dimly she heard more voices, and felt something bump her bed. Two green-coated attendants swam into view, rolled her onto the gurney and wheeled her out of the room, down a long hallway, into an elevator. She could hear voices fading in and out, laughter, noise, as she floated somewhere between awareness and oblivion.

Then she was left alone in what seemed to be a huge room lined with other gurneys and she dozed, letting the quiet and warmth wrap her in a comforting insulation. The next thing she was conscious of was being unceremoniously dumped onto a cold steel table with three enormous lights glaring above her. She heard voices around her and tried to focus but the cold and brightness and noise confused her.

"Joanna." A calm voice penetrated the blanket of swirling sensations. "I'm Dr. Jacobs." The surgeon pulled down his face mask and leaned closer so that she could recognize his distorted features. "We're ready to begin surgery now. Just take a deep breath when I ask you to." A hard rubber contraption was lowered over her face and Joanna inhaled the sharp sweet scent and the world went blank.

CHAPTER SEVENTEEN

Pete stood at the window of Joanna's room, staring at the street far below.

"Pete," Betsy repeated for the second time, "would you like Eve and me to bring you a sandwich or something from the cafeteria when we come back?"

He shook his head without turning around. "Thanks, I'm not hungry."

Betsy met Eve's eyes and shrugged. "Okay, if you're sure." She stood up and flexed her shoulders. "I'll be back real soon. And don't worry, Pete." She touched his arm in a comforting gesture. "Joanna will be all right."

"Yes." Eve added, "Marvella assured me the surgery would go well."

Betsy turned to Eve and said in a low voice, "I sure hope that psychic is on target on this one. I don't think Pete could handle it if anything happened to Joanna."

"He really cares for her a lot, doesn't he?" Eve said softly. "Makes you wonder why he didn't marry her years ago."

"He went into service, and Joanna's family moved away and they lost touch." Pete felt a wave of sadness sweep over him at Betsy's whispered words.

The two women left the room but he could still hear their voices as they stood waiting in the hallway for the elevator.

"I wish Pete would come with us. He needs to eat something. Hey, let's get him a carry-out."

"Good idea." Betsy giggled, reminding him of school days. "Maybe the two of us could force feed him."

"You'll have to do it alone, Betsy. I've got to drive to the airport and pick up Cliff. But I was hoping to hear from Joanna's surgery before I left the hospital. Shouldn't we have heard something by now?"

"I'd like to think no news is good news."

Pete glanced at his watch for the umpteenth time. "And so would I, Bets," he said aloud. "So would I."

The sound of the elevator arriving and doors opening and closing cut off the women's conversation.

After what seemed an eternity, he heard noise in the hallway and rushed to the door just as a gurney bumped off the elevator and Joanna was wheeled into her room. And when the orderlies rolled her onto the bed and she moaned, he had to ball his fists tightly to keep from flattening both of them.

"Joanna. Wake up, Joanna. You're back in your room now."

Her eyes opened but did not appear to focus. She made an obvious attempt to swallow and gagged.

"Okay, she's awake."

Joanna moved her lips but no sound came out. "I...hurt," she finally managed to whisper.

"What? What is it?" an orderly asked loudly.

Joanna repeated the words again.

"You hurt? Okay, babe, you can have a shot for the pain."

One man prepared the hypodermic needle and the other turned her to expose one bare hip. Pete cringed as the needle sank into her flesh but she didn't seem to notice the stick at all.

Then they were gone and he closed his hand over hers and spoke in a distinct voice to penetrate her drug-induced fog.

"Welcome back, Joanna. You're going to be okay. Just go to sleep now, I'll take care of you."

The sedative quickly took effect and Joanna drifted back to sleep. Pete sat beside her, watching her deep measured breathing, feeling a sense of relief that she had been returned to him.

Pete lost track of the time; he knew the gray light had turned to darkness, that Betsy and Eve had been and gone, that nurses came and went at scheduled intervals, as Joanna slept on.

He dozed in the warm room and woke with a start when a male voice spoke at the foot of the bed. "I'm Dr. Jacobs. Just checking on the patient. Has she been awake yet?"

"Only for a few minutes when they brought her in."

"That's good. The more she can rest, the better for healing."

"Doctor, what about the surgery?" Pete asked in a low voice.

"The tumor was the size of a tennis ball, and attached to the ovary. It was totally encapsulated and we got it all. And though her organs were in excellent condition for a woman who has given birth, I did a total hysterectomy just to avoid any further problems in that area."

Pete opened his mouth to question the doctor's mistaken assumption, but Dr. Jacobs continued.

"We've sent the tumor for biopsy. I have to warn you, there is a chance it will prove malignant."

"How soon...?"

"We should know something in a few days. I'll be checking back with you in the morning. Have them call if you need me sooner. Good night."

He sat in stunned silence, the doctor's words hammering against his heart. Biopsy. Malignant. *No God, not again. Not Joanna. Please God, no.* And then he recalled the other thing and realized that he had forgotten to question it. Could it be? Surely the doctor would not have been mistaken about that. But it couldn't be true. Could it?

Through the long night, Pete kept his vigil beside Joanna in the semi-darkened room, trying to comprehend the reality that he might lose her. He became aware of voices outside in the hallway and glanced at the luminous hands of his watch. He had not realized it was late enough for the changing of the guard, as he called the times when a new shift came on duty and nurses stopped and discussed the charts contained in small cubicles beside each patient's door.

When the voices moved on down the hall, he sat staring for a long moment at the metal door that accessed the records from inside the room. Pete hesitated, knowing what he was about to do was against hospital policy, but weighing ethics against his need to know, the scales tipped in favor of the latter.

Stealthily he crossed the room and pulled the chart from the cubicle. He stepped into the adjacent bathroom, closed the door and turned on the light. Most of the words on the clipped pages were scrawled in almost illegible handwriting, with abbreviations and terminology he couldn't decipher. But flipping through the thick sheaf of papers, he was finally able to ferret out what he sought and the hard facts hit him in the solar plexus like a blow. He put the material back and returned to his vigil beside Joanna's bed.

There was no denying Dr. Jacobs' words any longer. Joanna had given birth to a child. But why wouldn't she have told him? And why had she led him to believe there had been no other man in her life all these years? Had she married and divorced someone or was she widowed? And more importantly, where was her child? He could imagine removing all traces of a marital relationship for one reason or another but how could she erase all evidence of a child; why would she want to?

Joanna stirred and moaned softly and he looked at her dark tousled hair framing her face which was only a nebulous shadow. He had thought he knew her so well, but did he really?

"Pete?" she whispered faintly.

"Yes, my darling. I'm here." He took her hand and bent to kiss her cheek.

"I'm...thirsty."

"They say you can't have water yet, but I can give you chips of ice." He removed the top of the pitcher and transferred ice into a glass and spooned thin pieces onto her tongue.

When she was satisfied, she spoke again. "I...hurt."

He rang for the nurse who brought another injection for the pain and he sat holding her hand until she slept again. But through the long hours until dawn, there was no sleep for Pete. Over and over, he sifted the facts he knew and sought answers to his questions, but there were none. There was only one thing he was sure of and that was his unconditional love for this woman. And he knew that he would still want to be with her and take care of her regardless of the outcome of her medical tests and no matter what she told him about her past. Nothing could change that.

****

Joanna sat in the recliner, wrapped snugly in her burgundy velour robe with her white afghan draped over her knees. An open book lay in her lap but she, lost in thought, stared out the window at the darkening sky. Surely she would know something soon, probably tomorrow.

It had been three days since her surgery and the foggy aftermath of the anesthesia had gradually lifted; she was feeling almost normal again. It would be a few more days until her stitches came out and then she could go home. How nice it was to know that Betsy would be there to take care of her until she was feeling stronger. Pete had offered to stay, too, but she and Betsy had persuaded him that it would be better this way and he hadn't insisted.

Pete had been wonderful, staying with her through the nights, anticipating her needs before she could voice a request, but there had been something in his face that she hadn't seen before. A kind of watchfulness when he didn't know she was looking. And although he repeatedly told her that he loved her, she sensed a holding back that puzzled her. She sighed and opened the book. It was almost too dark to see the print but the cord for her light lay on her bedside table and she didn't want to change from her comfortable position to get it. She wondered what was keeping Pete. Perhaps the traffic was unusually heavy today.

"Forget to pay your light bill?" A teasing voice broke the silence and Joanna looked up quickly at the welcome sound. Pete stood in the doorway and she gave him a wry smile.

"I'm sure I've paid it well but I was too lazy to get out of my chair without someone here to force me."

"Confession is good for the soul." He crossed the room and bent to kiss her, reached for the light, hesitated, and hung up his coat instead. He came back to stand by the window, leaning his weight against the ledge. "Joanna, there's something I want us to talk about."

So it hadn't been her imagination. *Here it comes. The part about how he can't take this a second time. So long. It could have been so good between us. But I can't deal with more sickness.* Suddenly, she wondered if Dr. Jacobs had told Pete that she had cancer and he was going to tell her that now.

"Dr. Jacobs told me something that I think we need to talk about."

So that was it. She took a deep breath. She wouldn't cry. *God, please don't let me cry. Give me courage.*

"The night you came back from surgery, he...mentioned that you...had a child." Pete stopped and the words hung between them, an invisible barrier in the shadows.

For a moment Joanna didn't comprehend what Pete had said, so sure she had been of what he was going to tell her. Then comprehension dawned and she was mute, a million sensations whirling in her mind as she tried to think how to respond—denial, protest, apology, anger, accusation. Finally her frozen face moved and she whispered acknowledgement. "Yes."

"Why didn't you tell me, Joanna? I knew you weren't a virgin. I didn't expect you to have lived a nun's existence all these years. Why did you lie to me, tell me I was the only man you'd ever slept with?"

Joanna lifted her head and tried to read Pete's face but he was silhouetted against the waning light, his features invisible. She still didn't understand his words.

"Even we Catholics are broad-minded about divorce now if the circumstances warrant it. I assume it was divorce since you surely wouldn't have been ashamed to tell me you were widowed? But the thing I can't figure out is why you would deny your own child? I know you love children as much as I do, and surely you don't believe I would reject your child just because I wasn't the child's father?"

"You are my child's father," Joanna said quietly.

For a moment, Pete was speechless, then he said harshly, "Then why in God's name would you...?" He stopped, passed a hand across his forehead. "Joanna, please explain this."

Her ears were ringing and she thought she was going to faint and wished that she would. From far away, she heard a voice that was not her own but it was telling her story.

"I didn't know about...the baby until after you had gone. I wanted to tell you but you were already overseas and I didn't know how to reach you. My father was furious and he made me go to St. Louis, to a home, and he took another church in Tennessee, so that after...I never went back to Greenville. I...I wanted our baby, Pete, but I was scared and they all said I wouldn't be able to take care of a baby by myself and I should give it to a family who would love it and—"

"You gave our baby away?" Pete asked brokenly.

Too choked to speak, she nodded mutely. Then the anguished words spilled from her. "I loved our baby. She was beautiful. And I only had her for two days. *Two days*, Pete, was all I had to remember a lifetime. And as long as I live, I will think of her and look for her in the faces of every young girl I meet. I stare at your daughters and try to imagine how much she would look like them. And that's why I couldn't marry you. This would have been between us always. I couldn't tell you, I knew it would break your heart. But as long as you didn't know, I could enjoy your love and pretend it hadn't happened. But now you know—" Her voice was flat, expressionless. "—and you won't ever want to see me again."

He opened his mouth to speak but she held up

her hand to stop him. "I won't ask you to forgive me, I can't even forgive myself. But please believe that I loved our baby and I did what I thought was best for her."

In one swift movement, Pete was on the floor beside Joanna's chair, his face buried in her lap. "It is I who must ask forgiveness, Joanna. What have I done to you, to your life, to our child, and all because of one careless moment?" He took her hands, held them to his face. "If I'd had any idea of all this, I wouldn't have allowed your father's insults to keep me from finding you. I did look for you when I came home on leave, did you know that, Joanna?"

She shook her head. "My father never told me. But it wouldn't have mattered. I don't think I could have faced you then after what I'd done."

"Have you ever thought of looking for her since? There are agencies that try and find—"

"No, Pete. When I signed the adoption papers, I memorized the words I pledged to abide by." She took a deep breath, repeated slowly in the silent room, "I know that this is a final act by me and that I can never in the future revoke this instrument or claim any right or interest in the child or make any claim against the Society."

"But things are different now, Joanna. Children look for parents, and parents for children. Maybe—"

"I've given it a lot of thought, Pete. But Jennifer Bernadette would be thirty now. She has a life of her own and it doesn't include me."

"Jennifer Bernadette? You named her?"

"Yes, that's the name I put on her birth certificate though the social worker said her new family would probably call her something else. But she's still Jennifer Bernadette to me."

Pete pulled her to him, held her close, then said softly, "We can't unwish the past. I know it's too late to change anything for her, but I want you to marry me and let me try and make it up to you for all the pain I've caused. I've asked you before, but now I have another reason for wanting to take care of you and devote the rest of my life to making you happy."

"You would marry me now? Knowing that I gave our baby away?" Joanna asked in awe.

"You did the only thing you could do, Joanna. It was never your fault. The blame is all mine. Marry me, Joanna, as soon as you feel strong enough."

"No, Pete," Joanna answered. "My answer is still the same. Not because of this, but because I don't know what's going to happen to me, and if it's cancer, I can't put you through that again."

"Joanna, it doesn't make any difference whether you're my wife or not. I'll feel the same way about you in either case and I want to take care of you no matter what happens."

"Then let's leave it at that, Pete. I can't marry you now."

"All right. We'll talk about it later. Right now I want you to get back into bed and rest. Now wasn't a good time to put you through this, I know. If I'd had any idea..."

"I don't feel tired, Pete. I feel as if a heavy weight has been lifted off my shoulders." Joanna allowed Pete to pull her into his arms. "A weight I've carried all these years alone." He bent to cover her mouth with his and kissed her gently, rocked her back and forth with a soft crooning sound, as together for the first time they mourned their loss.

CHAPTER EIGHTEEN

The days of Joanna's hospital stay passed quickly with Pete's caring attention and cheerful visits from Betsy and Eve. She had little time to be apprehensive about the results of her biopsy but it remained an unspoken fear deep inside her.

She was sitting in the recliner by the window finishing her breakfast as Dr. Jacobs and a nurse entered. She put down her coffee cup and gave them a tentative smile.

"Good morning, Joanna. How do you feel?"

"Except for the gas pains and soreness, I feel fine, Doctor."

"A little more time will take care of that. I'd like you to lie down so I can take a look at those stitches now."

The nurse moved the tray and with her assistance, Joanna slowly got out of the chair and into bed.

She looked at the young blond woman who reminded her of someone she couldn't quite place. "I haven't seen you before, have I?"

"No, I've been off for a few days. I'm Beth Owensby," she indicated her name tag, "and I'll be your day nurse now." She adjusted Joanna's soft white gown so that Dr. Jacobs could examine the abdominal incision.

"Stitches look very good. I'd say they'll be

coming out in a couple more days and then you can go home." He pulled down the gown and patted her shoulder. "But I have even better news for you today." Joanna gave him her full attention, waited expectantly. "I've read your lab report. The biopsy showed no malignancy. It looks like we're free and clear on that one."

"Oh, thank you." Joanna blinked her eyes quickly to stop the tears she felt forming. "Thank you," she said again, and added a silent *thank you* to God.

He smiled at her. "You're a very lucky lady. Keep walking as much as you can. That will help both the problems you mentioned."

Dr. Jacobs turned to leave, seemed to realize that Beth Owensby was not behind him and turned back. She was standing beside the recliner holding the white afghan she had just retrieved from the floor where it had fallen when Joanna had returned to bed.

"Mrs. Owensby?"

"What—oh, yes, Dr. Jacobs. I'm coming."

The routine hospital activities occupied Joanna's attention until mid-morning. Now she welcomed a few moments reprieve as she sat savoring the beauty and fragrance of the dozen American Beauty roses that had just been delivered to her room. She reread the card lying in her hand, "I love you with all my heart, Pete." The words brought tears of happiness.

She had not given him credit for having the understanding he had shown. She had never imagined that Pete would forgive her, let alone still love her, when he found out what she had done. Now with Dr. Jacobs' good news she could make plans for her future—a future that included Pete.

"Pretty roses," her day nurse said as she returned carrying an armload of sheets and towels. "Someone must think you're very special." She glanced around at the other containers of assorted flowers and greeting cards. "A lot of people, I guess."

Joanna smiled. "They are cheerful, aren't they? I never realized how much cards and flowers meant until now."

"That's a pretty afghan, too," the nurse observed as she stripped the bed. "Did you crochet it yourself?"

"Goodness no, I'm all thumbs when it comes to needlework." Joanna smoothed the afghan lying on her lap. "But my mother made it."

The nurse, what was hee name? Beth. Joanna finally remembered. Beth spread the bottom sheet and tucked it under the mattress. "I've never seen another quite like it. What is that pattern?"

"It doesn't have a formal name. This is my mother's own variation of the Wagon Wheel pattern; she called it a Circle of Love."

The nurse left the other sheet half-folded on top of the bed and came closer to Joanna. "Is that a letter of the alphabet in the center?"

"Yes, it's an 'H'—her signature. My mother's name is Hope." Joanna fingered the soft white yarn.

The young woman stepped closer and touched the afghan. "Did she...ever make another one?"

"Oh, yes. Hundreds, I suppose. You see, she was a minister's wife, and she sat through hours of church meetings and used to spend the time crocheting."

"You must have a lot of them then?"

"No." Joanna shook her head. "She gave most of them away to new babies in the church, to old people in nursing homes, to needy families."

"I see." She turned back to the bed, slowly finished her task in silence. "I'll get some fresh ice water, then I'll help you with your shower."

Joanna sat looking after the pretty nurse as she left. Her resemblance to someone she knew still eluded her. Wait, it was Michael Damron. Yes, that was it. The same shade blond hair, same cheekbones. Only Michael's eyes were the startling blue of Pete's and this young woman had large brown eyes, more like her own. Now that she thought about it, the likeness between the nurse and Michael was remarkable.

Pete arrived shortly after her nurse departed and spent the remainder of the morning with her. The hospital staff had grown accustomed to his almost constant presence and always brought two trays so they could share mealtime together.

When they had finished eating, Pete removed her tray table and gently pulled her up and wrapped his arms around her. "I'm going to tuck you into bed for a nice, long nap while I check on some farm machinery I've ordered."

"In a little while," she answered. "Eve brought me the schedule for next semester and I want to look over it first."

"Are you sure it wouldn't be better to rest now and tackle work later when you are stronger, my love?"

She shook her head. "I'm like an old race horse, you know. Too much inactivity and I get restless. Besides, I'm feeling quite well today."

He pressed her closer and kissed her lips softly, then nuzzled her ear lobe. "You are not an old race horse. And I can scarcely wait until I have you back home so I can kiss you properly."

"Neither can I, Pete. It's been far too long. I've missed sleeping with you. In every sense of the word."

"There's plenty of time for that. We won't rush things, no matter how much I want you." He gently lowered her back into the chair. "And if we keep talking about things that arouse my libido, I won't be able to get my mind on business."

"Then go along, and hurry back. I'll miss you."

As Pete's steps echoed in the hallway and she heard the elevator doors open and close, she sighed happily. What had she done to deserve a second chance with this wonderful man she loved? She reached for her new class schedule and a lined pad and pen which Eve had thoughtfully provided and began scribbling notes.

She had not realized how easily she would tire after surgery and soon set aside her work and climbed back into bed. There was only another week until the next semester began and she hoped her recovery would be complete by then. Her advisees would be depending on her and she was determined not to let them down.

Her eyelids drooped and she napped until a light knock at the door awakened her. The day nurse entered the room and came to stand beside the bed, depositing a shopping bag she carried on the floor beside her.

Joanna pressed a button on the control panel, raising herself to a reclining position, and smiled.

"Nurse Woods said you went out to lunch today with your father. Did you enjoy the sunshine?"

"Very much." A short silence followed and then the young woman spoke again. "I—uh, I notice from your chart that you have a daughter. Does she live here in Memphis?"

Joanna did not answer immediately while many possible responses to this very personal question crossed through her mind. Finally, some compelling force caused her to tell the truth. "I—I don't know."

The young woman stood looking at her intently but did not speak. Finally, Joanna broke the silence.

"You see, I haven't seen her in a long time." She swallowed past the lump in her throat. "Not since she was a baby."

The nurse sat down on the side of the bed and

took Joanna's hand. "I...have something to ask you. It's very important to me that you tell me the truth."

"If I can." Joanna looked at the solemn girl and wondered what on earth was coming next.

"I...want to know about your baby, your little girl."

Where is this leading? Joanna was filled with a mounting concern. She hesitated a long moment before she answered. "All right."

"Was she...adopted?"

How could she know...but, of course, it wouldn't take a nursing degree to deduct that from the facts she had provided. *The question is, why does she want to know?*

After a long hesitation, Joanna answered, "Yes."

"What was her name?" Beth's strained voice was scarcely above a whisper.

Joanna's heart was pounding in her ears as she looked at Beth Owensby's expectant face. Her mouth felt stiff and she had difficulty forming the syllables. "Jennifer Bernadette. Are you my—"

Bending down, Beth pulled her own white afghan out of the bag on the floor, laid in on the bed between them. "I'm your daughter."

They both reached forward at the same time, embracing with a hunger born of all their years of separation. Words and tears and laughter mingled, none of it making sense but it didn't matter to either of them because now everything made sense. And finally, they just held each other, rocking, crooning, mumbling endearments as ancient as life itself.

And into this happy tearful reunion walked Pete. For a long moment he stood silently, unable to comprehend the significance of the scene. Then Joanna became aware of his presence, and she held out an arm to beckon him into their circle.

"Pete. Oh, Pete. She has found us. This is our Jennifer Bernadette."

Beth looked up in surprise. "You mean...?"

"Yes, darling." Joanna nodded happily. "This is the man I love, have always loved, the man who is your father."

Beth wept then, deep racking sobs, tears that showed her joy and surprise and relief. Finally, she looked from Joanna to Pete and whispered, "The last piece in my genetic puzzle is in place. Now I can have a child of my own."

As Pete sat on the foot of Joanna's bed, Beth between them, holding each of their hands, she tried to explain what led her to them.

"I grew up in a happy home, with two wonderful parents. But after I married Neil, who is a resident intern here—" Both Joanna and Pete nodded their approval as she went on. "—we began thinking about a family. But I wanted to find my birth parents because I needed to know what genetic history I had before committing to have a child."

"A wise decision," Pete said and Joanna knew he was thinking of his own grandchild and the challenges she and her parents would always face.

"My mother—" She looked at Joanna apologetically. "—my adoptive mother, was strongly opposed to that so I didn't try to find you until..." Here she stopped and brushed tears from her face. "She died in a car wreck several months ago."

Joanna squeezed her hand and Pete placed his free arm around her shoulders.

In a moment, she continued. "I had to start my search with no information. My father didn't want to betray my mother's wishes, and anyway, he felt I might be better off not knowing someone who had given me up to strangers."

Joanna started to protest, but Pete shook his head. "Later," he mouthed to her silently.

"For a while, I thought Daddy was probably right. I ran ads in newspapers and a woman answered, trying to convince me I was her child but all she really wanted was money."

"Oh, Beth," Joanna said in an agonized voice.

"And then I found out the state where I was born. And finally I learned, with no help from my father the lawyer, that I was of age to access my adoption papers."

"So that is how you found us?" Pete asked.

Beth shook her head. "It was not that simple. I learned my birth mother's name and address. Then I tried to find her through old school records but there was no one in the files with her name. So I finally had to admit defeat."

Joanna was openly crying now, hot tears streaming down her face. "That was because I used my mother's maiden name. I'm so sorry, darling."

"Then how—" Pete began.

"At Christmas, Daddy gave me the afghan he said I was wrapped in when he and mother got me from the adoption agency."

Joanna nodded. "A Circle of Love."

"And when I saw yours here this morning I began to suspect a connection. I wasn't truthful when I told you I'd never seen another like it." Beth gave Joanna a tremulous smile. "I had seen *one other* like it but I was afraid to hope."

"What are the odds of this happening?" Pete asked in awe.

"So I called Daddy and asked him to meet me for lunch. And strange to say, he told me what I needed to know even before I could ask him. It seems he had recently made the connection between the names himself."

"And that's when you came back with your own Circle of Love." Joanna wiped her eyes and beamed at her daughter, then Pete. "Can you believe this? I'm afraid I'm going to wake up any minute and find out it was a dream. Just think, our daughter is sitting here between us. Our Jennifer Bernadette, no, our *Beth*."

"I can't wait to tell Daddy that I've found *both* my birth parents." She looked at Pete. "He already knows you two but I don't think he has a clue what your relation to me might be."

"He knows us—" Joanna began in an uncertain voice.

"Yes, he dates your friend, Eve Whitfield."

"Cliff Averill," Joanna and Pete said in unison.

Joanna's mind went into reverse. That first meeting at the art exhibit. Eve saying he'd shown such an interest in her. The questions he'd asked at the nursing home. Her thoughts went to fast forward. If his interest had been in getting information to protect his daughter, how did Eve fit into the picture? Had he used her as a means to an end? She became aware that Pete was speaking and made an effort to focus on his words.

"Your mother and I have a lot to tell you, Beth, but I think we should let her rest first. How about waiting to hear our story tomorrow?"

"I'm sure I can wait one more day, since I've waited thirty years for this," Beth said with mock resignation. "And I really must get back to work now. My coworkers have been covering the floor for me too long as it is. I'll stop back to say goodbye when my shift is over."

She bent to kiss Joanna's cheek, then hesitantly looked at Pete. He wrapped her in a loving embrace and held her tightly for a long moment. "Don't disappear, sweetheart. You don't seem quite real yet, so we need to see you often to reinforce your presence."

"Don't worry. Nothing could keep me away. And if you don't mind, I'd like to have Neil come by tomorrow to hear your story."

"We'd welcome that," Pete assured her. "We

need to meet the man who thinks he's good enough for our daughter."

When Beth had gone, Pete turned to Joanna. "This must have been the reason you had to go through surgery."

"Yes, I suppose it was. If I hadn't come here now, I wonder if we would ever have found each other?"

"Maybe. Maybe not. And to think, all this time, you were both living right here in Memphis."

"Jenni—Beth may even have attended Memphis State. I may have passed her on campus. I must remember to ask her about that tomorrow."

"But for now, you are going to close your pretty eyes, eyes that I note our daughter has also, and try and rest. I'm afraid all the excitement may slow your recovery."

"Oh, no," Joanna assured him. "I feel such a sense of peace. I thought it would be enough to have found you again, but now to have our daughter, too. My life is complete."

CHAPTER NINETEEN

Beth stood beside Joanna's recliner, holding her hand. "I'm going to miss popping in to see you every day, Mom, but I'm glad Dr. Jacobs is dismissing you tomorrow."

"I have mixed feelings about leaving here because I'll miss seeing you, too, darling."

"Neil and I will be back for a visit tonight. Would you like to have dinner with us in the cafeteria, Dad?"

Dad. How that word warmed his heart. And just looking at the beautiful young woman who stood there in her crisp white uniform filled his heart to overflowing. "Thanks, but I'll just have a tray here with your mom as usual."

"Then I'll be going before traffic gets heavy. It will be so nice to move to Saddle Creek when Neil begins his practice and not have so far to drive."

"That's very generous of Cliff to give you two his house."

"Well, Daddy says it's way too large for him now and," she giggled," he's hoping we'll take the hint and fill it with grandchildren soon."

Pete put an arm around her. "Your mom and I are in total agreement with that. Come on, I'll walk you to your car."

Beth stooped to embrace her mother. "I think you should take a nap, Mom. I know you are feeling much stronger, but going home tomorrow will be stressful. Your body is still weak and needs time to heal."

Pete grinned at Joanna. "Listen to your nurse, my love. What she says makes sense to me."

As Pete and Beth stepped into the elevator, he asked, "Have you told Cliff—uh, your daddy—about me yet?"

"Yes, I told him at lunch today. But actually, I don't think he was surprised. He is an attorney, you know, and he had done a lot of sleuthing into my past."

Pete nodded. "In a effort to protect you."

"I can see that now but it was very frustrating to my search. He had discovered my mother and was debating whether he should tell me when I found out for myself. Thank goodness, he told me that very day I saw the afghan or I might not have forgiven him."

They left the elevator and walked toward the entrance before she spoke again. "Anyway, Daddy said he was almost certain about you after he saw Michael at Thanksgiving. Do we really look that much alike?"

"You could be twins except for different color eyes."

They made their way through the crowded parking garage to Beth's car and Pete opened the door and waited while she fastened her seat belt.

"Drive carefully, sweetheart." He bent to kiss her cheek.

"I will. See you tonight."

Pete stood looking after his daughter until the car disappeared in the labyrinth of darkness. *Surely my cup runneth over.* With a contented sigh, he turned back toward the hospital entrance.

As he approached the snack shop, redolent with the scent of cinnamon and brewing coffee, he recognized Eve Whitfield coming out the door with

Cliff Averill close behind her.

"Save it, Cliff. Don't waste any more of your Mister D. A. in the courtroom persuasion on me, because this is one juror who isn't buying."

He stepped back into an alcove leading to a lounge as she stormed past, eyes blazing. She raised her voice. "I feel used. Used and dirty."

Cliff reached out to touch her arm and she jerked it away as she hissed. "Don't touch me. Don't ever come near me again." With an elegant toss of her long hair, Eve flounced down the hallway, while Cliff watched her go, a miserable expression on his face.

"Christ, what have I done?" he asked aloud.

Pete shrank further into the shadows and Cliff passed by. *What the hell is going on?* Then it dawned on him. Cliff had dated Eve to learn about Joanna. And now she must have figured it out. No wonder the poor woman was hysterical. He debated whether to tell Joanna about what he'd seen but decided against it for now. Maybe it was only a lovers' quarrel and they would patch it up and none but he would be the wiser.

He pushed the button for the elevator. He and Joanna had much to talk about and plans to make for the future, their future together.

"Pete, wait for us."

He turned to see Betsy, Thelma, and Vada coming toward him. "Hey, what is this? Another high school reunion?" His broad smile included the three of them.

"Vada and Thel came over to see Joanna and we've been out to lunch," Betsy explained.

"You two go on up," Vada said. "I'd like to stop in the snack shop a minute with Pete." She looked at him quickly. "You don't mind, do you?"

"*He* won't mind, but wait until we tell Joanna." Thelma rolled her eyes. "Don't be long, hear?"

She and Betsy went on toward the elevator and Pete and Vada found an empty booth. The waitress came and they ordered coffee before Vada spoke again.

"Pete, I have something to tell you. I don't know how to say this except to just confess and say I'm sorry." Pete looked at her with a puzzled expression and she hurried on. "You see, everyone was upset about consolidating the elementary schools and a lot of them were blaming you for the merger." He nodded. "And rumors began to circulate about your ability to make decisions. Some of them had to do with your relationship with Joanna."

Pete's mouth was set in a straight line as he nodded again. "Well—" The steaming coffee came and Vada took a quick swallow and grimaced. "Al and I, well, we were some of the most vocal protesters against you."

"Everyone has a right to their opinion," Pete said with what he hoped was more charity than he was feeling.

"But that's not all." Vada twisted her napkin, and began shredding it into small segments. "I...took advantage of my friendship with Joanna. When she said you two had no intention of getting married, after you'd taken that trip to Branson and she was spending weekends at your house, well, I told Al and after the consolidation passed, he...started a petition asking for your resignation on moral grounds." Pete made a sound in his throat, but she held up her hand to silence him. "But when I heard about Joanna's surgery, I felt so bad about what I'd done that I told Al to stop that thing at once or I'd take out an ad in the Greenville Times and make a public apology." She wiped her eyes with a corner of the largest piece of napkin that remained. "I love Joanna, and I really am sorry, Pete. I guess I've always been a little bit jealous of her, though. I don't suppose you ever knew this, but I had a terrific crush on you in high school."

"But you and Al?"

She shook her head and smiled. "It was you I really wanted to date, captain of the basketball team, handsomest guy in school. But you never had eyes for anyone but Joanna. I went to the Flemmings' church then, you know, and I used to pray that Joanna's father would be transferred someplace else." She shrugged. "But it happened too late to help me because you were already gone by then."

"I never knew," Pete said quietly.

"Well, it's all right. Al is a great guy and we've had a good life together. And I never would have told you this but I thought it might help you to understand why I let the green-eyed monster take control of my tongue. All of a sudden, Joanna was back, looking better than ever, and you two were crazy about each other again and flaunting your affair for everyone to see."

"Well, just for the record, Joanna and I are planning to get married."

Vada's face registered surprise, then pleasure. "Oh, Pete, I'm so glad. Truly, I am. I've felt awful about what I did ever since I knew she might have cancer."

Pete nodded. "And we've got some more good news." He stood up. "Come on, let's go up and let Joanna tell you about that."

As he walked behind Vada toward the elevator, Pete shook his head in wonder. He would never in a million years have believed what she'd just told him if she hadn't been so obviously sincere. *You think you know people*, he mused, *but you never really know who is inside that facade you recognize.*

After the visitors had gone, Pete stayed on with Joanna, the two of them still basking in all the congratulations and good wishes on their upcoming wedding and Joanna's favorable report from the biopsy, but most of all sharing their still-private joy in the discovery of their daughter.

"I was dying to tell them about Beth," Joanna said, "but I really think the other children should be the first to know."

"I agree." Pete reached to take her hand. "And I'd like us to tell them together, about Beth and the wedding. So I guess we will have to keep our happy secret a little longer but I'd like to shout it from the rooftops."

"So would I." Joanna was silent a moment, then continued. "Pete, do you think the other children will mind? About Beth, I mean?"

Pete chuckled. "With five plus four inlaws already, what's one more? Seriously, though, I think they'll love having Beth for an older sister. After all, she was here first, they just didn't know about her."

"I hope you're right. Beth has told me how much she is looking forward to having brothers and sisters."

"Meanwhile, my love, I think we have some planning to do. Like when and where we want to be married. And where you want to go for our honeymoon."

"How does Easter weekend sound to you?"

"Tomorrow would be better." Pete grinned at her. "But I'll settle for that."

"I want to be married in St. Joseph's," Joanna said. "And I'd like Michael to perform the ceremony."

"But Joanna, that won't be possible since only Catholics are allowed to marry in the church," Pete explained carefully.

"I understand that," Joanna answered, "and I see no problem." At Pete's look of puzzlement, she added with deliberate nonchalance, "Since we both will be by that time."

"Joanna, are you sure?" Pete looked at her intently. "There's no reason to do that for me. After all, you'll be giving up so many things already—your position at the university, your condo, your life here in Memphis, even your opportunity to be near our daughter and your mother."

"I've thought it over carefully, Pete." Her voice was firm. "I want to do it, for both of us. I stopped going to church a long time ago. It was more a protest against my father than God. But now I want to be a part of something greater than myself again, and I always dreamed of marrying you and being a member of your church and the community. So I don't feel I'm making any kind of sacrifice to give up my condo, or my position at MSU."

Pete lifted her hand lying on the bed next to him and kissed it. "Joanna, you never cease to amaze me. Every time I think I couldn't be any happier, you add to my happiness even more."

She smiled at him and continued. "Beth will be looking in on my mother. With her medical training, she will be far more competent than I am to handle health issues. And I expect we'll visit Beth and Neil often and they'll also come to Greenville. Besides, if I were to stay here, I might become a nuisance to them trying to make up for all the lost time."

"You could never do that," Pete assured her. "It's obvious Beth wants all the time with us she can get. Isn't she a doll? Those beautiful brown eyes, just like her mother?"

"And so striking with your blond hair. Isn't it amazing how much she looks like Michael?"

"Yes, I noticed it right away," Pete agreed. "Well, looks like we've settled all the important things except our honeymoon. Any ideas on that?"

"How about a few days in Branson at the Grand Palace?"

"You've got it," Pete said quickly, then added,

"and in the fall we can take a real honeymoon to Europe or someplace since we won't be working when the crops are in."

"Pete, I never said I wouldn't work. I've been in the classroom so long I don't think I'd know what to do with myself if I weren't involved with students. I plan to look into teaching someplace if I can."

"It will be your choice, Joanna. You don't have to work, you know that, but I want you to do whatever makes you happy." He raised her hand, kissed her open palm. "And now I have a surprise for you. I've been thinking about the house and I've decided that I'd like to offer it to Kyle. Since Ursula is expecting again, they're going to need more room and I thought, well, this was the house Mary Esther and I...anyway, I'd like to build a new house for you, whatever plan you choose."

Joanna was silent a long moment before she spoke. "That's a very generous and thoughtful gesture, Pete, and I'm grateful for the offer but I really don't think we need a new house. I'd rather renovate your parents' home when Kyle and his family move out. I've always loved that place with its cupola and all those porches and I would enjoy redecorating and furnishing it. I can just imagine how beautiful that white Victorian two-story would be, refurbished with dark shutters and wrought-iron porch railings. So that's what I would prefer, if you don't mind?"

"Mind?" Pete chuckled. "You have just saved me enough money to pay for that trip we might take to Europe someday." He stood, bent to kiss her. "Now you need to get some rest before Beth comes back with our new son-in-law this evening. I think I'll go for a long walk and stop somewhere for a beer. I've had about all the surprises I can cope with these last few days. I need to spend some time processing all that's happened before my brain overloads. I'm just a farmer, remember, not used to living life in the fast lane."

Joanna returned his kiss with all the love she felt for him. "Hurry back."

"Hey," he mumbled huskily against her ear, "if you don't stop kissing me like that, I may change my mind and not leave at all. And I don't think that bed is wide enough for me to hold you the way I'd like."

"There's always tomorrow after I go home," Joanna whispered.

"I doubt it," Pete said wryly. "Nurse Betsy will probably guard her patient with an eagle eye until she feels you are fully recovered."

"Then I'll just have to get well fast," Joanna promised, "because I can't wait for you to sleep with me again, and I mean that romantically."

"We have plenty of time, my love." Pete bent to kiss her again. "We have all the time in the world."

CHAPTER TWENTY

It was a balmy day for mid-February and the early signs of spring were evident in the bright yellow just visible on the forsythia bushes and jonquils that lined the sidewalk leading into Oakwood Manor.

"I'm glad I waited till you were able to come with me, Mom," Beth said as she parked the car in front of the long building and went around the car to open the door for Joanna.

Watching her daughter cross in front of the car, Joanna smiled happily, and repeated the word "mom" softly. It was still hard to realize that she had her precious child back again after all these years. And Beth had solved the problem of what to call her by saying that she already had a mother and a daddy so she would call Joanna and Pete mom and dad. Pete's other children also called him dad but she supposed she would always be just Joanna to them.

As she got out of the car, Beth reached into the back and brought out a shopping bag Joanna recognized as the one she'd brought to the hospital with the afghan that matched her own.

"I thought she might remember it," Beth said shyly by way of explanation.

Joanna shook her head. "Don't be disappointed if she doesn't, honey. Your grandmother probably won't even recognize me."

A soft warm wind ruffled Joanna's hair as she walked slowly toward the tall columns flanking the entrance to the convalescent center. "It's almost spring," she said. "Soon these tall old trees will be leafed out and the tulip and crocus blooms will fill those flower beds."

"I think I'd like to plant some flowers this year," Beth mused, "if we move to Saddle Creek in time. My mother did a lot of gardening but Daddy has let the beds get all choked with weeds since she died."

Joanna was glad that Beth could talk of her adoptive mother without any constraint. She had encouraged her to do so, and it seemed to have enhanced their own relationship for Beth to share her memories of the woman who had reared her. She smiled as she answered, "And your grandmother loved to work in flowers also, so I guess you may have gotten your green thumb from two sources."

"Environment and heredity, which is most important?" Beth asked lightly as they entered the building.

"Both are of equal value in my book," Joanna answered with sincerity. "Come on, your grandmother's room is down this hall." She waved at a nurse at the desk in passing.

At the door to Hope Flemming's room, Joanna hesitated. "Maybe I'd better go in first, see how she is."

"Mother?" Joanna raised her voice slightly, as she walked toward the bed. "Mother, I've brought someone to see you. This is Jennifer Bernadette." They had agreed it would be better to use the only name by which Hope Flemming had ever known Beth.

The frail, white-haired woman's eyes flew open and she looked startled for a moment. Then Beth came forward and stood close beside the bed.

"Hello, Grandmother Hope." She took the thin blue-veined hand that lay limply on top of the cover and bent to kiss her wrinkled cheek. "I know you won't remember me, but maybe you'll remember something you made for me a long time ago." Beth pulled the afghan from the bag she carried and held it close so that her clouded eyes could see the signature in the center of the Circle of Love.

At first there was no response and then the hint of a smile hovered on her creased mouth. "Ba...bee?" she said faintly and then repeated with more certainty. "Ba...bee."

"Mom," Beth said in a choked voice, "she knows." She bent to hug the old woman, then stroked her hair as she said softly, "Thank you, Grandmother Hope. If you hadn't made this Circle of Love, I might never have found my mom or you again. Thank you."

Joanna brushed the tears from her own overflowing eyes. "Beth, I'm going to the lobby for a few minutes and check with the nurses about Grandmother's medicine. You can stay here with her if you like."

Beth sat down on the side of the bed and began talking to the woman she had already come to love, as if her grandmother's confused mind could understand all that she wanted to say. At the front desk, Joanna explained to the nurse that her daughter and son-in-law would be visiting from time to time. If the woman thought it strange that she had mentioned no other family members until now, she kept the thought to herself and Joanna offered no further explanation.

The phone rang while they were talking and when the nurse answered it, she looked at Joanna who had started back to her mother's room and motioned for her to wait. Putting her hand over the mouthpiece, she asked, "Is your daughter's name

Owensby?" Joanna nodded. "Then there's a call for her from her husband."

Joanna hurried to notify Beth, wondering why Neil would call her here when she'd been gone from home only a short time. Surely he would wait until she returned to get a report on how the visit had gone.

Joanna stayed with her mother while Beth rushed to answer. In only a moment, she was back. "We have to go; that call was about Daddy. He's been hurt. It had something to do with Eve and a protest march."

"Where is he now?"

"At Baptist Hospital. In emergency. Neil says he has a concussion and they're having to take stitches in his head." She bent to give her grandmother a hurried kiss. "Goodbye, Grandmother Hope. I'll be back soon. I love you." To Joanna, she added as she stuffed her afghan back into the bag. "Let's hurry. I can't believe this. I thought Daddy and Eve broke up so why would he be marching with her in a parade?"

Why indeed? Joanna could think of no answer as they walked toward the car, Beth several steps ahead in her determination to get to her beloved adoptive father as soon as she could.

****

"March is certainly roaring in like a lion." Betsy shivered as she came inside and hugged Joanna. "God, I must look like a witch."

"You look marvelous," Joanna told her. "And as for the rest of that old adage, I hope this means it will go out like a lamb and we'll have beautiful weather for our wedding."

Betsy laughed as she pulled off her lightweight navy wool coat and gave it to Joanna. "Pete has already placed a special order for that. And he knows people in high places."

"You mean Father Michael? I never thought of

that." Joanna motioned to her. "Come on in the kitchen. There's a fresh pot of coffee and I've made brownies."

"Getting domestic already, are we?" Betsy followed and settled onto a stool as Joanna served her. "I'm proud of you."

"Well, I did learn a few things in the kitchen while you were here. And brownies are Beth's favorite so I had to become an expert at them. I've got a lot of catching up to do."

"And you're loving every minute of it, I can see."

"I didn't dream this could ever happen now. To think that I've got Pete and our daughter both back after all this time."

"You deserve it, Joanna, after the hell your father put you through." She took a brownie from the plate, sampled it. "Hmm. Delicious."

Joanna nodded, then continued. "I used to hate him for what he'd done. But now that I have a grownup child of my own, I think I can see why he did it, even though I still think it was wrong." She sat down opposite Betsy at the counter and took a sip from her steaming coffee cup. "I don't want you to think that's why I'm converting to Pete's religion though."

Betsy smiled. "I never said a word."

"Well, I suppose it would seem logical. Get even with my father by doing the thing he'd hate the most."

"Your father is dead, Joanna," Betsy said in a practical tone of voice. "Are you taking instruction yet?"

"I'll begin next weekend when I go to Greenville. Pete has arranged weekend consultations with Father Saffer since St. Joseph's is where we'll attend church."

"Good idea. And if you need any help with your homework, you're looking at a woman who's coached seven children in learning their catechism."

"Thank you, Bets. And thanks for coming over to help me plan the wedding and shop for my dress."

"I wouldn't have missed it for the world. I've waited a long time for this wedding. Besides, I love shopping with you and Eve." She reached for the coffee pot and refilled her cup. "What time will she be getting here?"

Joanna looked at her watch. "Soon, I think. She had to check on Cliff first."

"At the hospital?"

"No, he went home yesterday. Beth and Neil moved on out to the Saddle Creek house to take care of him."

"God, what a show that must have been. He was lucky he didn't get killed."

"But I suppose the end results were worth it. Eve has agreed to marry him now. And—"

The door bell interrupted Joanna's words and she went to answer, returning with Eve moments later.

"Betsy, how good to see you again!" The two women embraced.

"And you look stunning." Eve shook her head in answer to Joanna's offer of refreshments and turned her attention back to Betsy. "What have you been up to?"

"Well—" Betsy paused for effect. "I do have some news but I was waiting to tell you both at the same time."

The two women looked at her expectantly. "Go on," they urged in unison.

"I have a job."

"How exciting. Where? Doing what? Have you started work yet?"

Betsy waited for Eve's barrage of questions to end before she answered. "Well, I've been wanting to go to work ever since I came to Memphis and saw how much fun career girls have, and I thought and thought about what I could do. And I finally decided to just do what I know best and I talked it over with Pete and he pulled a few strings and so I'm going to be a fraternity house mother at SEMO, that's Southeast Missouri State University, Eve."

"Oh, the college at Cape?" Eve asked and Betsy nodded.

"That's wonderful, Bets. When do you start?" Joanna asked.

"Summer term. And that's not all. I decided to sell the farm since I'll be living at the frat house and when I told Pete he made me an offer I couldn't refuse." She looked at Joanna. "Did he tell you already?"

Joanna shook her head. "Not a word."

"Good. I was afraid he'd spoil my surprise. Anyway, with St. Joseph's Elementary closing, Lana will be out of a job so she's going to St. Louis to work and share the twins' apartment. So there didn't seem to be any reason for me to stay in Greenville."

"Well, I'll be there." Joanna reminded her.

"Yeah, it would have been fun to be neighbors but I need to get on with my life, too. Cape isn't far and you can come and visit often and we'll have lunch together."

"I expect that won't be too difficult—" Joanna suppressed a smile. "—since I'll be at SEMO a few days each week myself."

"God, that's great."

"For everyone but me," Eve wailed. "I was hoping to persuade you to come to Memphis, Betsy."

Betsy looked at Eve and shook her head. "I do like Memphis but I decided I preferred a smaller town and besides, Tim and his family are there."

"A good choice, I'd say." Eve put an arm around her. "And don't forget you can come here and go on another shopping spree any time you want and—"

"Speaking of which," Joanna interrupted, "we'd better get this show on the road if we're going to find a wedding dress for the bride-to-be."

"One of the brides-to-be," Eve corrected her as the three women headed for the front door. "Have you realized that we're going to be related when these weddings take place, Joanna?"

"I hadn't thought about it but yes, I guess we will share the same family. And be grandmothers to the same babies." Joanna smiled as she locked the door. "That ought to be very interesting."

"If past performance is any indicator—" Betsy turned and winked at Joanna. "—it will be a riot."

CHAPTER TWENTY-ONE

Holy Saturday before Easter was perfect for a wedding, sunny, warm, filled with flowers and birdsong, a time of renewal. And Pete's crowded house reflected the mood of spring as all the family gathered before going to St. Joseph's for the ceremony.

In the guest bedroom Joanna put on her ivory silk two-piece dress and did the last-minute things common to all brides-to-be.

"Shall I fasten these for you now?" Betsy asked, taking the strand of large creamy pearls from the box on the dresser.

"Yes, please." Joanna smiled at her dearest friend who appeared almost as nervous as she felt. "Aren't they gorgeous?"

"Gorgeous." Betsy fumbled with the clasp, confirming Joanna's suspicions. "A fitting gift of love. There." She stood back to admire the bride. "I've truly never seen you look so beautiful."

"You look lovely, too, Bets. That pale blue is perfect with your eyes and hair."

"You-hoo. May I come in?" Eve Whitfield stood framed against the doorway, looking like a hyacinth in full bloom in her frothy lavender dress. "Have I missed all the preparations?"

"No, come in, you're just in time to help the bride with her veil," Betsy said.

"I'm sorry I'm late but Cliff and I..." She stopped and shrugged dramatically and the other two laughed indulgently.

"I take it Cliff is back to normal," Betsy said dryly.

"Better than ever, darling," Eve answered. "If I'd known he would recuperate so quickly I would have been tempted to make it a double wedding." She smiled to herself and added, "I think it may have been the ground damiana leaves I added to his diet."

Betsy laughed. "It was more likely the red-hot mama."

Eve nodded her head in agreement, then knitted her brows. "Of course, we would have had to marry in the parking lot instead of the sanctuary, I suppose, since I'm such a sinner."

"Well, maybe Father Michael would have at least allowed you to be wed on the front steps of St. Joseph's," Betsy teased.

"No matter. According to Marvella my horoscope says late June is the most suitable month to marry. And anyway, Cliff has promised me a honeymoon cruise to the Greek Isles, so it's worth waiting until the spring term ends to make it official."

"Wow," Betsy said. "You two make me think very seriously about looking for Mister Right myself."

Eve placed the veil on Joanna's head and adjusted the strands of hair around it. "How's the work on your house coming along, Joanna? Any more delays?"

"No, I'm sure it will be finished by the time my classes are over, so I'll definitely be out of the condo and Cliff can have possession by the first of June."

"Great. Cliff will be happy to have a place of his own again. He's looking forward to handing the keys to his house to Beth and Neil as soon as possible."

Betsy looked from Eve to Joanna. "Cliff is

moving into your condo?" Then back to Eve. "Till the wedding?"

"No, dear, permanently," Eve explained. "It's going to work out perfectly since it's only down the hall. We could never live together. He's a morning person, I'm a night owl; he prefers to read, I like TV; he's a neatnik, I function best in total chaos. We want to be married, but we each need our own space since the only place we're really compatible is in bed. And it is so inconvenient for him to drive all the way to Saddle Creek in the wee hours."

Betsy shook her head. "My God, that sheds a whole new light on marriage. Maybe I'll just look for a guy like Cliff."

"Lots of luck, sweetie, he's one in a million."

"And so is his fiancée," Joanna added with a smile.

"Mom, are you almost ready?" Beth stuck her head in the door and smiled at her mother. "Oh, you're beautiful."

"Thank you, honey." Joanna looked lovingly at her daughter, who wore a pale pink confection that reminded her of cotton candy. "And so are you."

The three women followed Beth into the den where the other family members, attired in full regalia, milled about with wine glasses in hand, talking and laughing in festive expectation.

Pete stepped forward and took Joanna's hands. "My beautiful bride," he said with a catch in his voice, then bent to kiss her softly. "I love you."

"Okay, everyone, listen now." Michael raised his voice above the din and a hush fell over the group. "Let's make sure we have everything in order." He pulled a folded sheet of paper from his pocket and consulted it as he spoke. "Thelma Bernard and Vada Mittendorf are attending the bride's book?"

"Right, they're already at the church," Betsy told him.

"Becky, do you and LaWanda have the reception under control?"

"Everything is ready," Rebecca said. "Dad and Mom and the wedding party will stay in the sanctuary for photos while the other guests move to the reception hall to be served. Ivana and Ursula will handle things alone until LaWanda and I can join them."

Joanna felt tears form in her eyes and she blinked them away. It wouldn't do for the bride to cry before her wedding but her heart overflowed with happiness. Pete's daughter had called her "mom" as naturally as if she had always been a part of the family.

"Okay, brothers mine, which of you groomsmen has the bride's ring?"

"I do," Richard answered.

"He always gets to do the good stuff," Kyle complained with a grin.

"Because I'm the oldest," Richard added and they all laughed.

Pete looked at his sons and shook his head. "Just like old times."

"And matrons of honor?" Michael looked around the room.

"Here." Eve waved a hand from where she stood beside Cliff.

"Me, too," Betsy added.

"And me," Beth said.

"And who has the groom's ring?"

"I do." Beth held up the ring as proof.

"So, all present and accounted for. Now—"

"You forgot the flower girl," LaWanda said, and pushed Robin forward.

"Well, so I did." Michael beamed at the little girl in her yellow ruffled dress with matching silk jonquils wound around her ponytail. "Robin, you stay with Beth and do what she tells you, just like at practice, okay?"

"Beff, okay." Robin gave Beth a happy smile and moved to her side and took her hand.

"Now," Michael continued, "I think a toast before the wedding might be in order."

Pete gave Joanna a wine glass, their hands touching as he did.

Even in this briefest of contact, she felt the current of his love flow from him to her.

"To the bride and groom. May they have a long and happy life together," Michael said and raised his glass and drank.

Pete stepped forward. "To all our family. May we be joined together in love." Pete drank the toast, then kissed Joanna amid the added wishes of the others.

"And to all our friends," Joanna added, and looked toward Betsy and Eve and Cliff.

"I propose we drink to our new mom and our new sister," Kyle said.

"And our new brother-in-law," Richard chimed in.

"And let me remind you that tomorrow I'll be christening Peter James Acree, another new member of our family," Michael added, "whose godparents are Beth and Neil."

"It must be contagious," Beth said, taking Neil's hand and stepping closer to Joanna and Pete, "because Neil and I are going to have a baby, too." She turned to her mother and added softly, "And if it's a girl, we're going to name her Jennifer Bernadette."

Joanna nodded, too full of joy to speak, and hugged her daughter to her. Pete's arms encircled them both as he said, "Well, if this one isn't, the next one is bound to be."

They drank another round of toasts to the new baby and the baby-to-be, and then Michael called out, "Enough. We've got a wedding to attend and I don't want it canceled because the wedding party celebrated too soon."

"I'll drink to that," Richard said, holding his glass aloft.

Kyle cuffed him good-naturedly on the shoulder. "To be continued at the reception."

"Time to go, everyone," Michael told them and there was mild pandemonium as the group divided up for the ride to the church.

Rebecca paused beside Joanna to discuss the last-minute reception plans and she took the opportunity to add, "Thank you, Becky, for making me feel so much a part of the family."

Rebecca looked first at her father, then at Joanna as she responded. "It is I who should thank you. All this time we've thought you were an imposter trying to take our mother's place. But now that we know about Beth, we realize it is we who were the real impostors. I hope you'll forgive us."

Joanna put her arm around Pete's daughter. "You're forgiven, on one condition." Both Becky and Pete looked surprised as they waited for her to explain. "I really can't cook very well, at least not without someone like Betsy in the kitchen to direct me. So since you are a Home Ec. teacher, I thought perhaps you'd not mind giving me a few instructions."

"I'd be happy to, and I'll share all our mother's recipes with you." She hesitated and looked as though she was afraid her words might have offended Joanna. "That is, if you—"

"That would be wonderful," Joanna assured her.

"Well, as long as Becky is giving instruction, I'd like to participate," Pete said. "After all, days when you're commuting to Cape in winter, I won't be busy on the farm, so there's no reason I can't make dinner."

"Hurry up, Becky," Lee called, "we're holding up the procession."

"Coming," she answered and with a quick kiss for both her father and future step-mother, she hurried toward the door.

Joanna and Pete rode alone in the new maroon Cadillac which had been another of Pete's wedding gifts for his bride.

As he turned onto the road that led into Greenville, he took her hand and they rode in silence for a time, following the possession of assorted vehicles in front of them.

"I love Betsy's new car," Joanna said as she returned the wave of the woman in the Toyota just ahead.

"That jaunty yellow car seems to suit her, doesn't it?" Pete observed. "At least, the new Betsy with the blond hair and the job at Cape. I'm glad to see her looking so happy for a change."

"Did you know she's going to Mass again?"

Pete looked surprised. "Betsy? I haven't seen her."

"Not to St. Joseph's. She's found a church at Cape near the college. Said she might as well make a fresh start at religion, too. She told me she hadn't realized how much she'd missed it until she began helping me with my own questions."

"Well, whatever it takes to make her happy."

"She deserves it," Joanna agreed.

"We all do," Pete added.

As they passed the school, Joanna glanced toward the parking lot. "Spring came early this year," she said softly. "Look, the pear tree is blooming."

"It's a good omen," Pete answered and lifted her hand and kissed it tenderly. "We've come full circle."

Joanna looked ahead, where friends and family were already gathering at St. Joseph's for the pledging of their wedding vows and knew with certainty that Pete was right.

God was smiling on the ever-widening circle of their love.

About the author...

Linda Swift is a native of Kentucky but has been a nomad all of her life. She currently lives in Florida with her real-life hero, a power plant consultant who keeps her "grounded." She is the misfit in a family of musicians which includes her husband as well as her son, daughter and son-in-law who live in Music City, USA. Even her precious Lhasa Apso granddog growls on key.

In her other life, she went to school forever and was a counselor and psychometrist in public education. "I would not have missed any of my life experiences," she says emphatically, "because they have given me the insight I need to write.

Linda has been writing since she was ten. She has had over one hundred poems, articles and short stories appear in a variety of publications and has won numerous awards for her work. WPSD-TV, an NBC affiliate. produced one of her plays. She is also the author of one other novel and a novella. Her passion has been writing novels since her first books were published in 1994.

Visit Linda at www.lindaswift.net

Also available from TWRP by Linda Swift:

LET NOTHING YOU DISMAY—December 2008